ROCK BAND FIGHTS EVIL #7

EARTH ANGEL

ROCK BAND FIGHTS EVIL #7

EARTH ANGEL

D.J. Butler

WordFire Press
Colorado Springs, Colorado

ISBN: 978-1-61475-392-6

Cover design by Janet McDonald

Art Director Kevin J. Anderson

Cover artwork images by Carter Reid

Book Design by RuneWright, LLC
www.RuneWright.com

Published by
WordFire Press, an imprint of
WordFire, Inc.
PO Box 1840
Monument CO 80132

Kevin J. Anderson & Rebecca Moesta, Publishers

WordFire Press Trade Paperback Edition July 2016
Printed in the USA
wordfirepress.com

Chapter One

It was the Chinese, I heard." The oldest of the three men picked through the garbage strewn on the asphalt around the dumpster, picking up abandoned syringes to eye them in the predawn light and sniffing discarded packages that had once held food. Finding a Ho-Ho wrapper with something in it worth harvesting, he turned slightly away from his companions and licked it clean with a withered tongue, careful not to let any crumbs fall on the cuffs of his jacket. He wore a tweedy sport coat with corduroy patches on the elbows, and his hair clearly hadn't seen a comb in weeks. "Heard it on the TV."

"TV from where? Chicago?" The heaviest of the three stood inside the dumpster, cracked and mismatched gumboots protecting his legs almost up to the knees. He shook a cracked plastic radio and listened to the rattle it made as if that would give him news. "You can't trust those bastards. You can't trust *any* of them. Besides, what would the Chinese be doing turning off our power? If it was the Chinese that wanted to get us, we'd have run out of cheap plastic toys and knockoff iPhones. Or maybe they'd have bombed us, I don't know, or gene-engineered a disease, but none of that ain't what happened. Shit just fell apart. I bet it was the government."

"You *always* think it's the government." The third man was rail-thin, stooped, and bald as an egg. He paddled through the sodden layer of refuse in the bottom of the dumpster with hands like spoons, stopping to examine avidly a treasure: a single, slightly cracked egg. "And it wasn't just the power."

A loud *crash* down the street sent all three men into huddled crouches, sheltering behind and inside the heavy, rusting iron dumpster. Curled red and orange leaves rustled, drifting into an ever deeper pile against the underside of a flipped pickup truck in the center of the intersection.

"Yeah?" The heavy man peeked over the edge of the receptacle. "Well, if you always think it's day, you're right half the time."

"Or you could just look at the sky." The old man cackled.

None of the three was a very good vessel; their hearts were full of fear, and the wrong kind. They weren't open to Heaven, and Raphael badly needed to find someone who was. And besides, they were scum. Even without society's collapse, these men would probably have been homeless drifters, the losers of life. This was how far Adam's children had fallen.

But despite the weight of the world crushing him, the Bearer of the Word couldn't pull himself away.

"It isn't just the lights, is it?" asked the thin man. "No mail, either. Disability check's gone, of course. Jack at the hardware store used to let me sweep up for him for a few bucks, but he pulled out two weeks ago and disappeared. Said kids kept stealing his stuff and the wholesalers had nothing to send to replace it. No one in Springfield was answering his calls and no one in Washington either; couldn't get a cop around to give him the time of day. Said money wasn't worth anything anymore anyway."

"See?" The heavy man was satisfied. "Government."

"That's idiotic," snorted the oldest. "The government doesn't do away with itself. It can't. Not in the nature of governments to do so. Never been a government I heard of yet that didn't make itself *bigger*."

"Yeah? What happened then, genius? You tell me."

The old man shrugged and sniffed a square of waxed paper that had once been wrapped around a stick of butter. "I dunno," he admitted, in between licking the paper around a greenish spot that might have been growing mold. "Everyone just went crazy. The country couldn't handle it—wasn't really built to handle it, I guess."

"Where'd Jack go?" the heavy man asked. "Chicago?"

"The Bull is strong." The thin man shook his head. "I dunno, mighta been St. Louis. I hear they got electricity there, off the river or something."

Another *crash*, and the three men ducked again. Down the street, a pack of teenagers jeered as one of them heaved a brick through a car window. It wasn't a theft in process; the rest of the car's windows were already gone. Mere vandalism. The exhausted wildness of drunks just before the dawn. Exultation in the spirit of destruction.

"Might make sense to follow him," the heavy man said thoughtfully. "I gotta tell you, I'm hungry enough to eat just about anything. I can already tell you what cat tastes like. And dog. No telling what might be next."

They don't know what they do, Raphael thought. Despite their fear, none of the men prayed. He turned and drifted through the air along the street.

It wasn't his fault. It wasn't his fault that the streets of this smallish Illinois town were thick with the weeping sores of damnation, invisible to the mortals among whom they oozed. Damned souls, released but not freed or healed by Jacob bar Azazel, Hell's new, upstart Lucifer, tortured each other in Raphael's plain sight. There had always been, he knew, a certain amount of ... overflow leakage. Occasional damned souls had always been able to be found upon the surface of the Earth by those who had the gift, or the curse, of sight. In recent years, in Dudael, he thought he had detected a small increase in their numbers. The approach of the Liminal Year, maybe.

But now they were everywhere.

And with them came suffering and rage.

It wasn't his fault. He had let Jacob take his father's hoof from its warded enclosure in New Mexico, yes, but this hadn't been his plan. Somehow—Raphael was unsure exactly how—Jacob bar Azazel had used that piece of his father's person to raze and harrow Hell. Now, even remembering the ponderous, dusty ache of millennia he had passed alone in the desert, Raphael almost wished he had remained faithful and stopped the rock and rollers from taking the hoof. Or turned a deaf ear to the Legate's wheedling. Still, this destruction was not what he had intended.

What had he intended? Now he wasn't sure. He liked to tell himself that he had wanted to turn the hoof back over to Heaven. He was a night watchman who wanted to let burglars in so he could catch them red-handed. Part of him doubted, but he ignored that part. Raphael had been tired of his long vigil, sitting for thousands of years on top of what amounted to little more than a fingernail clipping. A dangerous one, yes, but still a menial task.

He was destined, he knew, for better. Once, he had done better and greater things. Hadn't it been he who had brought judgment to the first murderer, Qayna, exiling her from humankind forever? Hadn't he also enforced the Writ against Azazel and his effronterous City of the Free? Raphael had been a great one, a trusted messenger of Heaven, and then he had been exiled every bit as much as Azazel, the grotesque leader astray of the hearts of multitudes.

And then an opportunity had fallen into Raphael's lap to take that bit of personal hygiene detritus and turn it into … at least a bargaining chip. Maybe more. Maybe even a weapon, or a tool with which to open the Stairway and return to Heaven.

Failure. He'd been defeated by a drunk, profane, trigger-happy band of bad musicians. *Not defeated*, he told himself. *Delayed.* They had forced him to make common cause with the Legate of Heaven, the sorcerer Pilate. Pilate, who had turned around and abandoned him in the rubble and riot of Hell as it fell to pieces around both their ears, leaving Raphael to fend for himself.

He considered letting the Veil drop, revealing himself to the rioting youths and soothing them with the Whisper of Eden. If there was anyone trying to sleep in this blasted burg, that might afford them a little more quiet, or at least it would allow the men exploring the dumpster's contents to do so in peace. But Raphael was tired and needed rest, and any peace he gave anyone would soon fade, and they didn't really deserve it anyway, so he passed them and continued up the street.

Around him, he thought, he should feel prayers. In early morning and late at night, on holy days, at prescribed times, these were the moments when the sons and daughters of Adam and Eve turned themselves towards Heaven, opening themselves up, at least a little bit, to powers they could not see. In Dudael he had gone years at a time without feeling a prayer, but then, he had gone years without hearing a human voice other than those of his own vessels. Here, among this desperate people, he expected to feel prayers in the dim light from all sides around him, through the walls. Instead, he detected nothing.

No, not nothing … there, not on this street but not far, he felt the gentle, vulnerable tremor that meant a heart had opened itself. At least one of these ungrateful wretches still remembered Heaven and turned to it.

He moved through backyards, drifting above sagging chain-link fences and hard-packed dirt where once there had been grass. Three houses in a row had burned to the ground completely, unrescued by either a Fire Department or any helpful neighbors. Feral cats still picked at the bones of someone who had died of a broken neck on the concrete pad behind one of the houses, having fallen out of the upper-story windows. A whip-thin basset hound whimpered and stared with liquid eyes, making Raphael wonder if it saw the blood-soaked orgy of tooth and nail before him, the damned torturing the damned.

Raphael saw the damned—at least, as long as he remained unveiled in flesh. Whether they saw him or not he couldn't say; they paid him no attention, scratching flesh from each other's bellies and drinking each other's blood. Though they looked like a crowd, Raphael moved among them easily. This was the geometry of the spirit: as a Bearer of the Word, he was a mere point. As a spirit only, or in the words of ancient Egypt that were still passed down among wizards like the Legate, a *ba*, one of the damned was also a mere point. The damned appeared to have substance and to be blocking the path, but with only one point and nothing draped over it, they were infinitely small. Raphael passed through them like one impossibly small gnat through a cloud of impossibly small gnats. Their eyes rolled back in their heads, they shuddered in the pleasure of their pain, and they ignored the angel in their midst.

His being a point didn't mean he couldn't interact physically with the world. It crushed him constantly, and it could also touch him, and, with the right weapons, even wound him. And he could touch physical things in return, though even small objects seemed to him to be massive. There was a paradox here and, frankly, understanding it was a little beneath him. Heaven had its engineers; he was a prince.

Maybe it had something to do with the weight of the world.

A Kwik-Pak store on Wise street. Blood on the shards of glass still clinging to the window frame. Burning damned upon the cracked and buckled sidewalk in front of it. But the prayer came from within. Far away, gunshots.

Screams.

Dear God, Raphael felt. *Dear God, help me.*

It wasn't a cry of terror. He went in.

Rats scurried across garbage-strewn tiles, sniffing at Twinkies boxes and Snickers wrappers and whimpering in frustrated anger. A short, mummified body lay stuffed into the corner under the hot dog broiler and the sink; no one had ever come to take away the corpse of the clerk who had died defending his store, though his gun and his pants had both been valuable enough for someone to steal. His shirt, crusted brown and full of neat round bullet holes, looters had so far left untouched.

Dear God, help me to do your will. Help me to find it today. Help me to survive, and to forward the cause of Heaven.

Raphael hesitated. In this ruin that had once been small-town Illinois, he was about to take away the one ray of hope he had encountered, depriving this person of will and the ability to do good.

But Raphael was so tired. The rough matter of Earth banged against him without a shielding body, bruising and draining him. He dared not return to Heaven or to the Queendom, and he didn't have the power to go anywhere else. Besides, what better purpose could this person serve than to be his vessel?

Dear God, make of me your vessel.

The praying man's words almost sounded like an invitation, and Raphael cast aside his doubts.

He found the man in the back of the shop. He huddled on his knees in what had once been an awkward nook created by the fact that the Kwik-Pak's freezer didn't quite reach the corner of the building. A collapsed stack of shelves and a tattered tarp shielded the praying man from view, but Raphael rose above the rubble and looked down at the man in his secret closet of prayer.

The praying man knelt on a scrap of army surplus wool blanket. He was young, maybe eighteen, with yellow hair and a face shaped like a fox's and a long-sleeved flannel shirt. He clutched his hands around a Gideon bible that had been torn in half. He twitched nervously as he prayed, and Raphael wondered if he were ill. Being inside any body was a limiting and unpleasant experience, made palatable only by the fact that, in Raphael's current situation, the alternative was worse. Being inside a sick body, or a wounded or dying one, was that much worse.

But the young man's soul was open. He was praying out loud, and now Raphael was close enough to hear the words and not just feel them.

"Dear God, keep me from harm if it's your will, but in any case let me be a sword in your hand, a shield for the suffering, a net to collect those who hunger for righteousness."

Raphael dropped the Veil.

"Child," he said.

The young man opened his eyes and gasped.

"Fear not," Raphael told him. The open warmth of the youth's spiritual being drew him like a candle drawing a moth.

"I ... I'm not afraid." The blond man managed an unsteady smile. "Are you a messenger?"

Raphael drifted closer, nodding. "I come with good tidings. I am here to make of you a vessel."

The young man said nothing, but opened his arms and closed his eyes. As was only right and proper.

Raphael embraced him. There was no act of will merging his substance into the vessel's body because Raphael had no will that was distinct from any other part of him. Raphael was a point, a ba only, or something like a ba. Being a point, he slid with ease and comfort inside the constellation of things that made up a living man. He entered through the man's name without being able to see it, but contact with the binding force of the five parts flooded Raphael with images of rocky hills and hickory trees, football games and math classes, magnolias in bloom and rain crashing on planted fields. Raphael nestled among the man's name, his body, his ka, and his ba, sliding about until the shadow that those parts cast became Raphael's shadow too, and he was a sixth point in the web of different objects that made up this man.

The scratching, thumping hardness of the world gentled as the flesh and bone of the man's body enveloped him, armored him, warmed him. He felt the now-shared heart set a rhythm for the world to which Raphael could dance within the interfolded parts of the vessel. Weariness fell away from his own limbs as he felt the young man's hungry, wiry, determined strength take its place.

Suddenly, he had lungs. He sucked in deep breaths and realized that the air was cold. Dizziness washed over his head in a wave, and Raphael fell forward onto his hands and knees. The relief he felt from the sensation of being squeezed and battered by the physical world almost hid the sudden pain in his hands as he scraped several knuckles in the cement floor and jammed one finger.

"Ouch," he murmured, but lay against the cool stone and let the pain simply be, reveling in the sensation of the chilled floor through the body's hot blood.

Eventually, he pushed himself back up onto his knees. Over long centuries of solitude in Dudael, he had dwelt in a series of bodies, some of them Anasazi, some Hopi, more than a few Spaniards, and eventually even Americans in all their complicated ethnicities. He didn't care about his vessel's race at all, but age mattered to him. He liked being in the body of a young person—not so young that he was a child, but old enough to be mobile in society without attracting attention. Young people moved faster, slept better, and hurt less, and the great crippling disadvantage of youth—utter, foolish ignorance—was one Raphael had shed many ages ago.

For only a moment, Raphael wondered what his vessel was experiencing.

Once, centuries before the people who would later be known as the Pueblo and the Anasazi ever came on the scene, he had dwelt in a vessel called Riplakish. After Raphael had moved his dwelling into a new, younger vessel, he had asked Riplakish what it had been like to host a Bearer of the Word. Riplakish had said that he didn't know. As far as he could tell, he had been asleep the entire time.

Though he'd had glorious dreams.

Raphael looked at the torn Bible in his hands. It was dog-eared, stained, and tattered, and the back had been ripped out, cutting away not only the entire New Testament but also ... Raphael did some quick reciting in his head, remembering the King James order of the books ... Malachi. He laughed out loud.

Malachi. The young man's Bible was missing the book whose title in Hebrew meant *My Angel.*

"Never mind," he said out loud. "You have an angel now."

He stood, joints aching a little from the cold despite his youth. He dug in the back pocket of his jeans and found a wallet. *Enoch Emery,* he read on the driver's license. *Tennessee.* No cash, not that it mattered.

There was a gun, though. A little black .357 snub-nosed pistol in a leather holster looped on his belt behind his back.

Raphael tucked the half-Bible into a back pocket and checked the handgun; it was loaded and well-kept, and Enoch had a handful of bullets in another pocket of his jeans. Raphael was not an expert in firearms, but he knew enough; he had dwelt in the body of a rancher in the 1890s, and one of his recent vessels, Mordechai Feldman, had been a United States Marine before he became a rabbi.

Raphael put the weapon back and moved into the front of the store. The street outside was light now with the coming of morning, but he didn't see any movement, so he risked a stop at the sink and turned the knob. The pipes groaned, coughed, and then began to pour out freezing water. Raphael washed his new hands and face, aware that one of the downsides of his body was that it smelled bad.

Though these days, everyone did.

Raphael washed up as best he could, there being no mirror in the Kwik-Pak. He realized he was hungry and he looked at a rat scurrying across a dusty shelf. The rat was fatter than his mortal vessel, had glossier hair, and looked altogether healthier. Still, it was a rat. Deciding against taking the risk of illness, he tightened Enoch's belt a notch and crept out into the morning.

In Enoch Emery's body, looking through the young man's eyes, Raphael could no longer see the damned infesting the streets. Escaping that sight had not been the point of entering the vessel, but it was definitely a benefit.

Raphael sighed. He had been rootless since the harrowing of Hell, and he had no plan. He had no destination. Raphael was an outcast. He had raised his hand against Heaven's will, and as a result, however good his justification might be, however mitigating his circumstances, he was homeless, a wanderer on the earth. He didn't dare face the Chancellor, but that didn't make him a coward—it only spoke well of his common sense.

He surveyed the scorched, rotting, plundered, dilapidated houses of the street and considered.

Maybe the desert, he thought. He had lived alone before and could do it again. An experienced man could always find food, even in the desert, and live off the land. He didn't dare risk going to Dudael, but the American Southwest was big and mostly empty. A man could hide, even from madness, for a long, long time.

"Raphael."

The voice from behind took him by surprise. Raphael wheeled around, hands up. Only when he was facing the other man did he remember that he had a gun and drawing it might have been a sensible move.

Too late.

The other man was older than Enoch. He was shorter, too, square-shouldered, straight-backed, with deep wrinkles around his eyes though the rest of his round face was smooth-skinned. His hair was ragged and black, but the thin, scraggly hair of his beard was nearly white. He wore a waistcoat over a puffy-sleeved shirt that looked a century out of style, though Raphael was no confident judge of fashion. The stranger extended one hand, offering to shake.

Tattooed onto the man's wrist, above his thumb, was a seven-branched tree.

Chapter Two

Raphael hesitated.

"Happy is the man that findeth wisdom," the stranger said, "and the man that getteth understanding."

It had been a long time since anyone had greeted Raphael this way. It took him a moment to find the response. "For the merchandise of it is better than the merchandise of silver, and the gain thereof than fine gold," he finally said.

He took the stranger's hand in a firm handshake.

The man raised his eyebrows politely, as if they were discussing a weather forecast, and didn't let go of Raphael's hand. "She is more precious than rubies: and all the things thou canst desire are not to be compared unto her. Length of days is in her right hand; and in her left hand riches and honor."

"Her ways are ways of pleasantness, and all her paths are peace. She is a tree of life to them that lay hold upon her: and happy is every one that retaineth her." Raphael crooked one finger inside the handshake, and the stranger crooked his counterpart finger in the same way in response.

"I'm John," he said, and released Raphael's hand. "The Prester."

Raphael didn't know what to say, so he said nothing.

"It's been a long time, hasn't it?"

Raphael looked around the street, wondering who might be watching from cover. Yellow light spilled onto the east side of the neighborhood's ruins, spattering over rooftops to give the crumbling structures momentary haloes.

"Mort Feldman was a Brother," Raphael said. "That's how long it's been. Not long at all, really, for those of us who do not fade and die."

"Ah, yes." The Prester's eyes twinkled. "And when did you meet my friend Mort?"

"Thirty years ago. We didn't talk much, after the first. After he became my vessel."

"Of course."

Raphael squinted at the Prester. What did he mean, *of course?* "Are you a Bearer of the Word?" he asked.

John shook his head. "No. But once, a long time ago, I was vessel for one and dreamed the dream of Heaven."

"Before you became a Son of Light?"

"After, as it happens. Does it matter?" John took Raphael by the elbow and turned him up the street. "Walk with me."

Raphael's thoughts raced. He had been inducted as one of the first Sons of Light centuries ago—*millennia*—but his exile in Dudael—his *service*—meant that he'd had precious little contact with other Sons for a long time.

"Is Enoch Emery a Son of Light?" Raphael asked.

"Newly inducted," John told him. "Anointed with the Spirit of the Lord only."

The first of the seven anointings. "But his hand isn't marked."

"Neither is yours."

"Mine can't be. I'm a Messenger, and ordinary ink will leave no mark on me."

"His couldn't be, either. He needed to lure in a Messenger, and we feared that ink on his skin might frighten you off."

"A Messenger?"

"Not just any Messenger. *You.*"

Raphael stopped walking. Ahead of him, a lean mutt with hair falling out in patches trotted out from behind a fallen log, stared at him, and growled. He drew back his shoulders to stand as tall and proud as this vessel's body would let him.

"What is my punishment to be?"

The Prester turned Raphael by the shoulders and looked up into his eyes. "Raphael," he said, "I'm not here to punish you."

Raphael looked down at Enoch Emery's feet, noticing for the first time the brown leather work boots. "Good. I do not deserve to be punished."

"Yes, you do. We all do. And none of us escapes a whipping. But none of us gets the whipping he really deserves."

Raphael sighed and gestured around him with his arms. The mangy dog yelped, looked over its shoulder, and scurried away. "This is not all my fault."

"Not all." The Prester put his hands in his pockets and looked around at the rot and ruin. "You made choices that helped lead us here. So did many other people. That's usually the way of things in the world."

"In the world?"

"There is a place where only Heaven's choices matter."

"Of course."

Raphael heard a heavy rattle of chain link and turned to look. The three clowns from the dumpster hopped and clambered their way over a weed-choked lot's fence and walked in his direction. They fanned out slightly as they came, like an army that marched to encircle. The heavy one held a splintered piece of two-by-four in one hand; the thin one held a short length of lead pipe; the old one held a steak knife.

"Are these men Brothers?" Raphael asked.

"Do you plan to ask them?" John stepped back, behind Raphael.

The Bearer of the Word inside Enoch Emery considered the advancing men. Their eyes sparkled in the sunlight. They were filthy, rumpled and armed.

They had blood on their mouths.

The shots, he thought. *The screams.*

He Whispered.

"Calm down," he urged the men. "Release your anger and be comforted." Even through the body of the Son of Light

Enoch Emery, he felt the warm winds of Eden blow, scented with myrrh and bdellium, tasting of frankincense, shining to his eyes like gold. The Whisper of Eden tired him, but to any son or daughter of Eve and Adam, the call to return to the natural home of the spirit was nearly irresistible. "Join with me in peace."

The heavy man bellowed and charged.

Raphael ducked under a swing of the two-by-four; this was another reason to be happy he was in a young, fit body. He jumped upward with both feet, slamming his shoulder into the heavy man's solar plexus and throwing him backward, staggering.

It wasn't just that Enoch was young and fit. The indwelling presence of a Bearer of the Word made any human vessel capable of feats of great strength, if only for a little while and at the cost of great exhaustion.

The men attacking him must be mad. Even being damned didn't necessarily make you resistant to the Whisper; if anything, a profound sense of loss and alienation from Heaven might make you more susceptible. But if your soul was broken—if you were insane, well and truly destroyed—you could be beyond the reach of Eden.

The other two men closed in on Raphael, right and left. He grabbed the half-Bible in his back pocket and hurled it like a weapon into the face of the oldest attacker. He nailed the man right between the eyes with the broken book. With Enoch's enhanced strength, the force of the blow knocked the target over backwards.

Raphael didn't want to shoot any of the men. He was a Bearer of the Word, not a Bearer of the Sword, and killing was not his calling. Killing was beneath him, if he could at all avoid it. Besides, something about his interrupted conversation with the Prester filled him with a feeling he couldn't quite articulate. The Prester hadn't come to punish him, so why *had* he come?

Raphael leaped over his downed attacker, stepping hard between the older man's shoulder blades to keep him down. Raphael looked for a weapon. He didn't find one, and hands empty, he spun around to meet the thin man with the lead pipe.

He didn't particularly want Enoch Emery to die, either, but that was the risk he decided to take. After all, Enoch had welcomed him. He had invited Raphael to take that chance.

Raphael raised his balled fists to punch the onrushing cannibal—

"*Hypno hymas deo!*" the Prester called, throwing a handful of glittering sand about him in a cloud—

The man with the pipe collapsed, crumpling limp into the dry gutter at Raphael's feet. His weapon rattled and banged twenty feet up the street. The heavy man, just beginning to clamber again to his feet, fell back flat, and the old man with the knife lay still.

All three instantly began to snore.

Raphael unwound his fists. "Thanks."

John put his hands back in his pockets. "I'm not here for thanks," he said. "I'm not here to rescue you. I'm also not here to punish you."

"Okay," Raphael said, "I'll bite. What are you here for?"

"To bring you a vessel."

Raphael arched a skeptical eyebrow at the Prester. "That can't be all."

John pulled a hand out of his pocket, and it jingled. "And to give you a car."

Raphael reached out slowly and took the keys. The Prester turned to point out a badly battered avocado-green coupe across the street. Raphael wanted to believe that the Sons of Light, after years of no contact, had decided to simply bring him a car and a body, but he wasn't that arrogant. "What's the catch?" he muttered.

The Prester shrugged. "The catch is that it's a Datsun 510. It's old, and its maintenance has been hit and miss."

"I'm older," Raphael told him, "and my maintenance has been atrocious. Besides, I'm not a car guy and I can't afford to be picky. Really, what's the catch?"

"No catch. The car is yours, and the tank is full. You can take it and do what you want, go wherever you want."

"But … ?"

"No but."

"Okay … *and?*"

"And I also have a commission."

"An errand."

"You are a Messenger."

Raphael weighed the keys in his hand and considered. "Where does this … commission come from?"

"You can refuse it. The car is yours."

Raphael frowned, but he pocketed the car keys. "Okay. Who wants an errand done?"

"Heaven." The Prester smiled. "Who else?"

"Do you mean … the *Legate* of Heaven?" The Legate had badly wanted to infiltrate the Sons of Light, and by now he just might have done it.

Dogs barked and somewhere in town a siren sounded.

"I mean Heaven."

"Since when has Heaven used the Sons of Light to communicate with its Messengers?"

"Are you Heaven's Messenger, then?" John looked at Raphael keenly.

Raphael felt his shoulders sag. He bowed his head. Was this a test? He had to say something, had to explain himself. "I've sinned."

"Pride."

Raphael nodded. He didn't quite believe it, but it was what Heaven wanted to hear.

"You have will," John said. "All beings with will sin."

Raphael looked at him. It sounded like his wandering days were over. Heaven might admit him again. "Can all beings with will repent?"

"Yes, if they meet the condition."

"What condition?"

"A penitent sinner must allow others to repent as well."

"And is there atonement? Is there healing?"

"Ah." John chuckled. "That is the issue. That is precisely the problem."

"You didn't answer my other question."

"No?"

"Why does Heaven communicate to me by the Sons of Light?"

John smiled. "We have been Heaven's from the first. We have been the watchers in secret, the runners of errands that could never be known. Now we are the redundant part of the network. The backup plan."

"The backup plan for what?"

"As with any backup plan, for when the main plan goes awry. I am a messenger because Heaven cannot trust all of its own these days."

"You mean the Legate," Raphael said.

"And his third."

"Is he right about that? A third of the Host of Heaven follows him?"

"I don't know. If not a third, in any case there are many."

"If you are Heaven's second network," Raphael asked, "why do you need me at all? Why not carry out the errand yourself?"

As soon as he had formulated the question, he knew what the answer had to be.

The Prester smiled. "You must Bear the Word."

"A prophet is to be called?"

"A man of vision has stood in the council of the divine ones."

"In Heaven?"

"Not that council."

Raphael thought back to the scene of chaos and destruction in the depths of Hell a few weeks earlier. He remembered watching the Legate of Heaven and the guitar player Eddie Marlowe running deeper into the caverns together while he was forced back. "Eddie Marlowe," he said. "You mean me to Bear the Word to Eddie Marlowe."

"Not I. Heaven."

Raphael was astounded. "What is he to do? Is there a king to be challenged? A president?"

The Prester shrugged. "I don't know. All I'm doing is bringing you the Word."

"Why me? I'm a sinner, you said so yourself."

"We're all sinners," John said. "And I don't question Heaven's instructions. I just carry them out."

Raphael laughed dryly. "Touché."

"Perhaps your isolation over the last few millennia makes Heaven believe it can trust you. Perhaps Heaven believes you are prepared to repent and again Bear the Word."

"I am prepared."

"We'll find out." The Prester extended a hand, palm up. In it lay a scrap of parchment, red and black characters inked on it on both sides.

Raphael tried not to show it, but his borrowed heart raced in joyous victory. To Bear the Word again, to be the Messenger who called a prophet. He made himself hesitate modestly, and then a terrible thought struck him.

He couldn't accept.

The Prester had identified Raphael's sin as pride. What this Son of Light thought, Heaven must also believe. Probably Heaven told him. Raphael couldn't accept this Word and Bear it, because—he could admit it to himself—he would do so out of pride. The Word would fail, he would again have worsened his already black name, and whatever chance he had of returning to Heaven would be gone.

He dropped his hand to his side.

"Is there a problem?" John asked.

Raphael's ensorcelled attackers snored. A motor revved in the distance. Two men in hoodies lurched into view, shuffling through the leaves piled up on the battered sidewalk.

"I'm not worthy," Raphael said slowly. In some sense he said the words because he knew he must, but the words shamed him, and as he heard them, he knew they were true. Without meaning to, he shed a tear.

"Great God of Heaven." The Prester chuckled, a friendly, open sound. "Who is?"

"But I ..."

"Please," John said, his chuckle collapsing into a flat, earnest face. "I know you're thinking of yourself and trying not to accept this Word for the wrong reasons. Stop. Accept the Word. Accept it humbly if you can; accept it from pride if you must, but at all costs, accept it. *There is no one else.* Accept it, for Heaven's sake."

He held out the parchment again.

There was no one else. The words knocked something loose for Raphael, and he sighed. He forced away from his thoughts all question about why he was doing what he did. There was no alternative. He took the Word.

Heaven needed him.

The Word was larger in his hands than he remembered. He looked down at in wonder, unable to read the mystic, secret characters that were neatly written in columns up and down the parchment.

John looked pointedly over his shoulder at the approaching men in hoodies. "Please, Bearer," he said.

Raphael put the parchment in his mouth.

It didn't dissolve instantly, as it would have had he not been inside the vessel Enoch Emery. Instead it slowly pulped into a mash, bitter, grainy, and thick. As it dissolved, he felt his being—his whole being, his combined with Enoch's—fill with light. He carefully kept his mouth closed to keep the light inside, sucking at the parchment and smashing it against his palate with his tongue until it was gone.

The men with hoodies stopped. They were squinting at the Datsun and whispering to each other. They looked around and their eyes fell on John and Raphael.

"Where do I find him?" Raphael asked the Prester.

The Prester's eyes widened in surprise. "Doesn't the Word lead you to him?"

"It can," Raphael agreed, "but I have eaten the Word, and I have no insight, no sense of where to go."

"Hey!" called one of the men in hoodies. "This your car?"

The Prester ignored the question. "I don't know," he said. "I know that after the meeting of the Infernal Council, Eddie

Marlowe returned to earth among the ruins of Ainok with three companions. They were all injured, but especially the Child of Mab."

"Twitch," Raphael remembered. "Who is a horse and a bird."

"No ordinary hospital will have any ability to treat such wounds to such a person." The Prester arched an eyebrow at Raphael.

"The Sisters of Nauvoo."

"Hey, assholes!" The hoodies walked closer. The one in the lead gestured wildly with both arms, but the second followed behind, hands in his hoodie's pocket. He looked like he had a gun. "I'm gonna take this car now, and we can do it one of two ways. You can be dead, or you can be alive. Either way, you stay here on this sidewalk and we drive away. Now, what say you gimme the keys?"

Raphael turned to face them. The Word was completely dissolved in his mouth, its light absorbed into his body. "Stop," he Whispered.

The warm wind of Eden blew across the faces of the two men in hoodies. The Prester chuckled.

"I … I …" The would-be car thief's gestures grew small and then stopped, and his eyes glazed.

"There is no car here for you," Raphael said. "Leave, and find your car elsewhere."

The frankincense wind of Eden blew, and the two men rolled away before it like dried-up leaves.

When Raphael turned back to say farewell to the Prester, the little man was gone.

Chapter Three

The interior of the Datsun was shabby, its upholstery frayed and its dashboard and steering wheel cracked. This was not a vintage car someone had lovingly restored—it was a car that had been driven long and hard, then tossed into a corner and forgotten. It smelled of dust, sweat, and especially gasoline.

There was a pile of stuff in the shotgun seat. Raphael sat and locked the door, looked around to be sure no one was approaching the Datsun, and then examined the pile. Pocketknife, cans of Sterno, MREs, space blankets, bottled water; it was a jumble, but a jumble of things that might come in handy.

On the floor in the back was a gas can. That accounted for the smell.

Despite the gasoline reek, the sight of the MREs made Raphael hungry. No wonder, given the Whispering and the feats of physical strength he'd performed in such a short time in this vessel. He forced himself to ignore the gnawing in his stomach.

Thinking of useful things, Raphael pulled the .357 from its holster and tucked it underneath his seat. He found a crack where he could wedge it in so it wouldn't rattle around but where it would be within reach.

Hunger aside, he felt good. He was Bearing the Word again after so many years, as was his due. And he would be the one to call a new prophet, the first in … he didn't know how long. This was much more important than guarding Azazel's hoof fragment. It was at least as important as Raphael's task of guarding Azazel himself or capturing the Prince of Ainok in the first place. Of course Heaven had come to him. He was the obvious choice.

Raphael caught himself and laughed a laugh of self-puncturing mockery.

"Don't forget," he said out loud, "Heaven only sent for you because they had no one else."

But he didn't really believe it.

With a few cold, rusty-sounding coughs, he managed to start the car.

He didn't know the way to Nauvoo. He had seen it last before the Flood, when it had been an encampment of the people of Shet, and Shet's daughters had there raised their Pavilion of Light as a place of healing, an alternative to the sickening "freedom" of the people of Ainok down the river. He'd certainly never driven there on American highways.

In the shotgun seat jumble he found a couple of maps. Interstate 55 looked like the fastest road, he thought, and he pointed the Datsun in that direction.

He passed ravaged churches, a smoldering Family Dollar store, and craters marking the sites of blasted buildings that could no longer be identified. People crept from ruin to ruin, keeping their bodies low and their faces hidden. Some were foragers or hunters, looking for food among the rubble with sacks and nets. Others, more obviously armed, looked for the foragers and hunters.

None of them molested him, and he didn't see another car in motion.

Over the freeway ramp hung a banner. On a bent metal flagpole whose concrete foundation had been yanked right out of the ground somewhere else and leaned up against the low freeway wall, hung a bull's head. It wasn't a real one but had been stitched together from cow hides, with big ragged holes torn out for eyes and rough-hewn wooden horns.

The ramp was blocked by a waist-high line of rubble except for a gap wide enough for one car. In the gap was parked a pickup truck. Along the line of rubble stood men with rifles. One of them wore a sagging leather bull's-head mask.

Never mind.

Raphael stopped the car and looked over his shoulder to back up.

As he looked back, he saw three men run across the road and lay down something that might have been a telephone pole. They stood behind the pole, hands on rifles and pistols.

I could leave Enoch, Raphael thought. He could abandon the vessel and take the Word to Nauvoo by himself.

But he didn't relish the idea of being again exposed to the crude material world of earth in his refined spirit self. And really, he had no idea whether he would find Eddie Marlowe at Nauvoo, or if he would even find any trace of the man. Nauvoo was a guess, and the road might be long ahead of him, and Raphael had no idea when he'd again find a good vessel. The people of Illinois seemed to have given up on prayer. Without a vessel, the weight of the world would eventually cripple him.

And most of all, he thought he shouldn't abandon the vessel. It was one thing to take a risk with the man's life, especially since he was a Son of Light and a volunteer. It was another to simply cast him to his death.

Bull Head swaggered over to the Datsun. He was a broad man, big bellied, in a white T-shirt and jeans. Raphael rolled down his window and smiled, keeping his smile fixed even as Bull Head made a wide-kneed, swaying dance move and snorted like an animal.

"Fifty-five belongs to the Bull!" Bull Head bellowed, thumping his own chest with the stock of his shotgun.

"Yamayol?"

Bull Head shook his horns in surprise. "The Bull of his Mother is great in the morning," he huffed to Raphael.

More passwords.

"I thought Yamayol was in Chicago," Raphael said, remembering the talk of the three men in the dumpster.

"The Bull of his Mother is great in the morning," Bull Head repeated.

Raphael sighed. He looked around for a way out but didn't see one.

"I'm not a follower of Yamayol," he said. "Can I pay a toll to use the road?"

Bull Head chuckled.

"Can I just go back the way I came?"

Bull Head leaned over the windshield to scrutinize the contents of the Datsun. "You can get out of the car and leave it here. I may let you live."

Raphael was tired, but he was out of choices. He Whispered.

"This car is pleasant and warm," he said, relaxing as the smells of Eden filled his human lungs. "Come get in the car with me, and together we will go home."

Warm golden light shone into the mask's eye sockets. Bull Head straightened to his impressive full height in a quick jerk, and for a moment Raphael thought the man was going to shoot him.

"Come with me."

Bull Head looked around at his men. They were too far away to hear Raphael's words, and they hooted and jeered, egging their leader on.

"I'm going with this guy," Bull Head called, his voice thick and slow. He walked around to the other side of the car, and Raphael threw things in the back to clear the seat. He kept one of the MREs, pinching it between his own knees. Bull Head opened his door.

One of the men stepped forward from the barricade, uncertain. "Hank?"

Raphael smiled at him. "Let's go for a drive, Hank," he said, feeling the warm, dry wind. He also felt a stab in the stomach of raw, violent hunger, and he trembled with effort. He was tired, his vessel was tired and hungry, and maintaining the Whisper of Eden required serious energy.

He didn't know long he could last.

"I'm going with this guy, Bill," Bull Head Hank said to his underling. "Now get out of the way, all of you."

Raphael tried to turn the winds on the underling Bill, while keeping Hank attuned. "I'm taking Hank for a drive—"

As he said it, he felt the wind grow cold. Pain seized the vessel's body, and he grabbed the steering wheel with both hands to steady himself. He clawed at the MRE in his lap, ripping the brown plastic to get at the contents. Bill stared at him.

Hank hesitated in the door, confused. Raphael tore open a disk that turned out to be an oatmeal cookie and jammed the whole thing in his mouth.

"What's … going on?" Bull Head Hank asked. He sounded like a child dazed from over-medication.

"Please sit down," Raphael Whispered. He blew cookie crumbs all over the steering wheel, but the sudden burst of energy from the food was enough. The wind blew again, and Bull Head Hank sat down. Raphael wished he could see Bull Head's face, but the mask hid everything. He was conscious of the man's shotgun, which he laid on the floor between his seat and the door.

"Get out of the way!" Bull Head bellowed again to his subordinates, and they did.

Raphael jammed the car into first gear and turned a tight, shuddering circle, tearing with his teeth at a packet whose label he didn't have time to read and then sucking something out of it that might have been beef stew.

"Water," he croaked.

Hank nodded and handed him a bottle. The horns of his mask gouged furrows in the Datsun's ceiling. "Where are we going?"

"Not the highway." Raphael slurped water like an animal. He Whispered again, just a little, just enough to keep Hank compliant. "We'll take a scenic route."

The Whisper felt cool, though, the fuel he was taking into his body either already burned or not being absorbed fast enough.

Hank was silent. Raphael shifted into second with a trembling hand and checked the rearview mirror; the Bull's men stood, perplexed, at their freeway tollgate, staring after him as he left.

He turned and shifted gears again. He needed to get out of sight fast.

"What's going on?" Bull Head Hank asked. His voice was harder and sharper.

"Have some food." Raphael tried to Whisper, but the winds didn't come. He shivered, feeling feverish.

"You tricked me."

"No, I …" Raphael looked over his shoulder; the freeway was out of sight, hidden behind an empty muffler shop. He shifted into fourth gear and let his hand drift downward.

Hank head-butted Raphael. The Bearer of the Word wasn't expecting it, and he also hadn't realized that the leather mask hid a metal plate above the eyes. The sudden iron thump to his temple made Raphael see stars, and the car swerved left.

"Wizard!" Hank roared and head-butted again.

Raphael shrugged a shoulder up over his neck and cringed away from the blow. Instead of the metal plate in the bull's forehead, this time he took a horn in the ear. Shrieking, he struggled to keep the car on the road, but he didn't let up on the gas.

Now was not a good time to get caught by Hank's men.

"Stop the car!" Hank grabbed Raphael by the throat.

At least he didn't go for the shotgun.

Raphael reached under the seat and felt his fingers close around the cold grip of the snub-nose. He jerked the wheel, trying to dislodge his attacker, but Hank only squeezed harder. He pushed in vain with his shoulder, and Hank laughed.

Finally, he pulled the pistol from under the seat and jammed it up against Hank's throat.

"Do it!" Hank roared, shaking him. "Do it!"

Raphael grunted with pain, took aim, and squeezed the trigger—

Not into Hank's neck, but into his shoulder.

He didn't hear the shot over Hank's yelling and the oxygen-deprived buzzing in his own ears, but Bull Head Hank suddenly sat back.

Raphael sucked in air, trying to stay conscious.

"Son of a bitch," Hank muttered. "That hurts."

Raphael's vision through Enoch's eyes swam, but he pushed the muzzle of the .357 against Hank's jaw. "Go for the shotgun," he warned the man in the bull mask, "and it'll hurt worse."

"You won't get away with this."

"None of us does. Take off the mask."

Raphael didn't care about the mask, but if he was going to be head-butted again, he preferred it to be without a metal plate loading the punch. Hank grumbled, but he slowly pulled the leather bag forward and off his face.

Without his mask, though, Bull Head Hank looked totally ordinary. His blocky head was mostly bald, his eyes small and piggish, and his jowls were prickly with stubble. He looked like a guy who watched a lot of football on TV and drank a lot of beer, and who hadn't slept enough recently.

Ironic, Raphael thought. Without his own mask of the vessel Enoch Emery, he would look entirely *extra*ordinary to Hank.

Or would he? What did these followers of the Bull of Chicago know, and what had they seen?

"What are you going to do with me?" Hank growled.

"I'm going to let you out," Raphael said. He switched gun hands and slowed to a stop in front of a field of dead yellow grass. "Take off your shoes and leave the shotgun."

With a gun pointed at him and blood dripping from his shoulder, Hank obeyed. Raphael watched the big-bellied man fall away in his rearview mirror, laughing out loud as the Bull's blockade captain gave him a surly finger.

A sense of decorum restrained him from giving the man a finger in return.

* * *

Raphael crossed a small river and drove west out of town, trusting to the Mississippi River to keep him from going too far. To the south, a scudding gray haze of smoke marked the presence of some huge fire he couldn't see, and when he could, he turned away from the fire and drifted north as well as west, sticking to two-lane rural highways.

Some of the fields he passed had been harvested, but many lay in rot. After passing three derelict gas stations, he tried an abandoned farm and had better luck there, siphoning gas from a John Deere tractor that lay tipped over on its side under splintered lumber in a barn behind the house. He had plenty of gas in the tank and can still, but he had no idea how far he really had to go.

He ate three of the MREs before he finally felt recovered. The slightly sulfuric tang of the bloated, gritty spaghetti stayed with him even after he ate two preservative-flavored brownie bars and swallowed thirty-two ounces of water.

He scanned through the airwaves twice, AM and FM both, and found nothing.

Raphael skirted around Carthage. A horseshoe nailed to a sign three miles outside of town might not have been a banner like the bulls' heads of Interstate 55, but Raphael preferred safe to sorry.

Nauvoo lay mostly on flat land barely higher than the river. It was a tiny town, and though Raphael hadn't seen it in centuries, he wasn't surprised at either its small size or at the high share of dreamers, reformers, and spiritual eccentrics he knew it had attracted by reputation in its not quite two centuries of modern history. Above most of the town and east of it, on a hill overlooking the Mississippi, stood the reason why.

It looked like a mansion, like the sprawling pseudo-Greek, semi-gothic, self-indulgent residence of some nineteenth-century robber baron, complete with a folly tower that faced the rising sun. Within it, Raphael remembered, hidden by all the ornate architecture, was the Pavilion.

He parked the Datsun, closed his eyes, and remembered how it had looked when Ainok had been the only city on what was now the North American continent. The pennants of the Daughters of Shet had snapped bravely in the sun. Mastodons and great ground sloths had grazed in the background, providing food for the people of Shet as they came here for healing.

He left all the weapons in the car and locked it. Unlike other towns he'd passed through, Nauvoo didn't look burned out and reduced to rubble. Maybe his things would be safe here, and in any case, he couldn't knock on the door packing heat.

The door was easily twenty feet tall and six wide. There was no knocker, so Raphael tapped on the polished dark wood with his knuckles.

A square he hadn't noticed in the door's paneling opened, filling with a woman's face of indeterminate age. Dark brown hair framed her cheekbones and forehead, pulled behind her ears and under a bonnet. She looked him up and down.

"I'm not ill," he told her.

"No," she agreed, "but you're not well, either."

"I'm here for something else."

"Do you have a right to enter?"

"Happy is the man that findeth wisdom," Raphael said, "and the man that getteth understanding."

Her eyes sharpened into a squint. "Show me your hands."

He held them out, palms up.

"Play the fool again and we're done."

"I'm sorry." Raphael wanted to kick himself. He thought she'd wanted to be sure he was unarmed. Instead, she wanted to see his tattoo.

She shook her head. "You lie."

"Wait!"

She hesitated. "Give me a reason."

Raphael relaxed, took a deep breath to prepare Enoch's body, and then emerged, Veil down and visible.

The solidity of the world pressed upon him instantly. "I don't bear the ink on my flesh," he said, "but I am a Son of Light." He drifted slightly away from the stone walls of the building, seeing the structure flicker white in the light that emanated from him.

Enoch Emery crumpled to the earth.

The gatekeeper eyed him thoughtfully. "What do you want, Bearer?"

For a moment, Raphael imagined that she could see the Word within him, and he swelled with pleasure at being known. When he realized she couldn't possibly see it and was just addressing him generally as a Messenger, he felt slightly scorned.

"I'm looking for the man Eddie Marlowe," he said. "He may be traveling in the company of the Marked Woman, Qayna, and another."

"If I did see him," the gatekeeper said slowly, "why should I tell you? A Messenger alone upon the face of the earth could be an outcast or in league with the Fallen, especially in these times." Raphael's annoyance mounted as the woman expressed her doubt. "You claim to be a Son of Light, but your vessel is not marked. Who are you to command me?"

Raphael trembled with rage. "I am the archangel Raphael," he thundered, "Bearer of the Word."

On the ground below him, Enoch Emery struggled to stand, clutching at the air and croaking. Raphael saw the man weak and off balance and thought of him praying, deliberately opening himself up to be a vessel for Raphael. He hesitated.

The gatekeeper arched an eyebrow at him.

"I am Raphael," he said again, this time with a quieter voice, and hands demurely at his side, though it cost him a great effort. "And I am begging you to help."

The gatekeeper looked from Raphael to Enoch Emery and back, then nodded. "We tried to heal the Child of Mab, but we failed. She's too broken even for our arts. They left us two weeks ago."

Raphael felt crushed. He had failed. He had no way to find them now.

"When we couldn't heal the fairy. Marlowe asked who else might be able to, and we told him there are no greater healers than the Daughters of Shet."

"Thank you," Raphael mumbled. The world around him battered him with its weight. It dragged at him, and he wanted to throw himself on the grass and let it simply crush him out of existence. There was to be no glory for him, no return in triumph having Borne the Word to the first prophet on earth in centuries. It was over. He would prefer not to exist.

Maybe he could find the Marked Woman and talk her into shooting him.

"He therefore vowed that he would dress the fairy in the Skin of Adam."

Raphael looked up sharply. "What?"

"Unnh," Enoch Emery groaned, falling back to the ground. "Can I get something to eat?"

Chapter Four

Enoch Emery cooked rice in a battered tin pot over one of the Sterno cans. The Datsun and a fallen tree kept the tiny light from the highway, but so long as Raphael stayed out of his vessel with the Veil withdrawn, it hardly mattered. He himself was a towering white column of flame that would be visible for miles around to anyone who looked.

Around them in the trees, the damned gibbered and moaned. Enoch saw nothing, of course, and Raphael did his best to ignore the sight.

"We must do this quickly," he told the young man with the fox-shaped head. It wasn't the damned that worried him, though. It was the possibility—the eventual certainty—of being seen by an unfriendly party.

Enoch slammed back the last of his second bottle of Gatorade and belched. "Thank you," he said, and pulled the sleeve of his flannel shirt back to expose his wrist.

"Are you sure?" Raphael asked.

"You're not my paralemptor." The man said the words peacefully, but there was rebar inside them. "I've been anointed, and now I want to be marked."

"Perhaps it would be good to continue to operate incognito."

"I agree. Also, perhaps it would be good to be able to be identified by other Sons of Light. Perhaps it would be good to be able to get help from people who want to help me. Us."

Enoch knew what had happened at the Pavilion because the same Daughters of Shet who gave him the Gatorade and a few other supplies had told him.

"Why are you doing this?" The sight of Enoch guzzling Gatorade brought home to Raphael that the Son of Light was paying a price for his help.

Enoch frowned as if the question were stupid. "I swore an oath. Didn't you?"

Raphael nodded. He picked up the pot of ink and the bone needle. They weighed tons in his hand.

"Besides," Enoch added, "it's the end of the world. What else am I gonna do?"

"This will not fade." Raphael dipped the needle and pressed it into Enoch Emery's wrist, beginning to trace the pattern that would mark the man as the Son of Light he was. "This stylus is the bone of Abil," he said.

"You know you're the only one," the vessel said.

"You have made an acceptable sacrifice of your heart, Enoch Emery." Raphael postponed any feeling of self-importance at the remark until he knew what Enoch was talking about. "Only one what?" He had completed the tree's stylized roots and began working on the trunk.

"You're the only Bearer of the Word to be anointed as a Son of Light."

"The bone records the worthiness of your deed." Raphael remembered inking the skin of the girl Qayna as the men of her family held her down. She had fled weeping, and later, Raphael, Qayna's father, and her brother Shet had convened in a dark forest and Raphael had marked the two men with the same tree with which he now marked Enoch Emery, and they had anointed each other with myrrh-scented oil from the trees of Eden. The deed had been part of Raphael's instructions in respect to Qayna with no explanation. Heaven rarely explained itself. "That was a long time ago."

"You've spent most of the years since then in the desert, haven't you?" The trunk of the tree was fully formed, and Raphael began to tease out its branches. "You must remember those times like they were yesterday."

"Though you be a vagabond and a fugitive upon the earth, these strokes record your name in the rolls of a new family, within whose tents there will always be place for you." He paused. "They *were* yesterday. Your perspective needs to be broader, Son of Light."

"I get it," Enoch said. "I played a little ball in high school, but I always told myself not to get a big head about it, and no matter what, not to let those be the glory days. You know."

Raphael resisted the temptation to stab Enoch. "I was in the desert," the Bearer of the Word reminded his vessel, "not on the dark side of the moon."

The young man snorted. "For most of those years, I don't imagine there was all that much difference between the two." He nodded admiringly as the final strokes of the tree took shape.

"This mark is yours, as you are theirs, until the end of time." Raphael finished the tattoo of the tree. "You don't know what the world was like before television," he told Enoch Emery, "but I do. I know how to be alone with my thoughts."

The vessel rubbed at the skin around the fresh tattoo. "I like television. Does that make me a bad guy?"

Raphael set down the ink and stylus, relieved to be able to lay aside the weight. "I like television too," he said. "Television is a powerful tool for telling stories, and sometimes stories are all we have. Except reality TV. I hate reality TV. Reality TV is for morons who want neither life nor truth, only the comforting clang of tinkling cymbals and sounding brass."

Enoch Emery nodded. "Well, the crash killed it all anyway. No more TV of any kind, really. Not that I've seen. You ready?"

"Yes." Raphael rose slightly into the air and looked around, seeing only the moon-silvered path of the river and the skeletal trees of late autumn. "I have heard the Bull still broadcasts on television."

"And go easy on the … what did you call it? The Whisper?"

"I will," Raphael said. "I must. It exhausts me."

"Yeah, well, it makes me feel like I have a toothache in my entire body. So keep it to a minimum."

Raphael ignored the sight of a woman in tattered rags smashing her own forehead against a boulder. "It hurts me too."

Enoch chuckled. "That ain't the right thing to say."

"No?"

Enoch shook his head. "Nope. The right thing to say is, 'Thank you, Enoch Emery.'"

"Yes, of course. Thank you." It pricked Raphael slightly to thank the vessel. "Only I thought you had your own reasons for doing this."

Enoch Emery must have thought that was funny, because he laughed hard. Then he knelt down and started to pray.

He said mighty prayers. The first syllables opened the young man to Heaven immediately. About him, the blooded and howling damned stepped back a pace. Without waiting for any further invitation, Raphael slipped through Enoch's name and into the vessel.

* * *

"Azazel is making trouble."

Kokhabel had caught him in the Hall of Snow, a glittering white arcade whose dazzling crystalline ceiling, it was said, had been the inspiration and model for the winter skies of Eden.

"Do you mean *more* trouble?" Azazel had been cast out of the Courts of Heaven many celestial turns earlier. Years, as the children of Shet measured time. Decades.

"He and his followers are doing strange things in Nod."

Raphael had heard of the strange things that were going on in Nod. He had other sources of information than the overeager Kokhabel. "Perhaps the Chancellor should hear," he suggested. "Perhaps a Writ might issue."

Kokhabel nodded and followed Raphael out of the Hall of Snow and into the Hall of Lightning. They both shimmered a brighter gold as they passed among the flashes of celestial brilliance. Another Bearer passed them both, nodding, on his way to fulfill some commission or answer some summons.

"I would like to know how to be of help."

"You would like to know how to come before the Throne and be made an Archangel."

"Is that so bad? I wish to serve Heaven."

"Archangels are created, not promoted."

"Maybe … maybe there are other ways of serving. Special callings for special crises. I don't need recognition."

The presumptuous little grasper thought he knew about the Sons of Light. Raphael almost laughed. "Then serve in your place. Heaven needs messengers."

"But I … I want to do more."

Raphael stopped. "Of course you do. Tell the Chancellor," he suggested, and looked Kokhabel in the face.

"I … I don't know that I have enough information. Maybe I'm wrong. Maybe it's too soon for a Writ to issue."

"Oh? What information do you have, then?" Raphael moved closer to Kokhabel, so close it was uncomfortable. It felt like the tingling space between them would force him to attack the other Messenger. That was deliberate; he wanted Kokhabel to back down.

"Rumors." Kokhabel shook his head and drifted away a handspan. "People have seen things."

"What people?" Raphael moved in closer again.

"People." Kokhabel gestured vaguely. "I want to help. Let me help you."

"Talk to the Chancellor," Raphael repeated. "You must excuse me; I have matters to which I must attend." He turned and left.

From the Hall of Lightning, the Bearer of the Word passed through the streaked Gallery of Rain and across the bare Courtyard of the Twelve Winds, all bathed in the white light of Heaven. He stuck to open spaces and chambers with abundant reflective surfaces so that he could see behind himself without turning and know whether he was being followed.

At the edge of the Mountain, he heard the voice of Shet calling him, and he Descended. Something troubled him in the Descent—something felt wrong, and he couldn't quite identify what it was. Kokhabel's prying, probably. The Bearer wanted to get above his station, to be an Archangel, to meddle in the affairs of Chancery. His was to bear messages only, to return and report. Who did he think he was?

He arrived in a tall tent filled with incense. Shet stood at the coal-filled brazier, arms raised. Beside him watched one of his sons.

"Happy is the man that findeth wisdom," Shet chanted.

It was not a mere formality. Raphael gave the countersigns.

"We have a journey before us," Shet warned. "Enosh is prepared to be your vessel."

Shet's son, Enosh, was tall and muscular. He bore the necessary tattoo on his wrist and a long scar up the outside of one arm. At Shet's words, Enosh promptly knelt and began to pray. Raphael nodded and entered the Son of Light. Within the incense-filled tent he felt fine, but he knew that emerging from it would immediately subject him to the weary pain of the world, a dull, grinding, monotonous pressure that must eventually reduce him to helplessness.

"Thank you, Shet." Enosh was strong and long-limbed, and if Raphael had to be within a vessel, this was a good one.

"Did you come alone?" Shet asked, eyes narrowing.

Raphael snorted at the preposterousness of the question. "Am I a fool?"

Shet shook his head dumbly and lifted the tent flap.

The night air outside was cool. Shet's tent was pitched on the highest ridge of a mountain peak, as was appropriate. Above, a fresh white moon smiled upon them, nearly full. They mounted two roan horses, and Raphael followed Shet down, down a long sloping ridge into a narrow canyon that led down into a broad valley. A low saddle connected the first valley with a second, and in the saddle, men with spears nodded at Shet as he passed. At the bottom of the second valley, Shet turned and led Raphael along a slow, shallow river. Enosh's body rode without effort and didn't tire. He had excellent balance and reflexes and strong arms. Raphael wondered what had been quick enough and dangerous enough to leave the long scar up the outside of the young man's arm.

Finally, in a grove of pine trees, Raphael heard the hooting of an owl.

Shet reined in his horse and hooted back, drawing a long knife as he did so.

A short man detached himself from the trees. Raphael didn't recognize him, and he didn't dress like the people of Shet, in animal skins or wool. He wore silk, and despite several layers of the fabric draped about him, he shivered in the night.

"Happy is the man …" The man in the trees gave the sign, and Raphael stepped forward to give the countersign. Shet and the newcomer showed each other the tree-shaped tattoos on their wrists.

"Enosh … ?" the man asked, eyeing Raphael closely.

"Enosh is but my vessel," Raphael said. "I am Raphael, Archangel and Bearer of the Word."

"Jared."

"*The one who descends.*"

"An honest enough name for a spy from the mountains who sneaks among the people of the plain. And you're *God's healer.* What does it mean?"

"I am a Messenger. I don't have a name in the same way that the children of men have names. *Raphael* is a label, though it serves well enough."

"And Jared is not my name, as the children of men have names," Jared said. "It too is a label, and it serves well enough."

"And what do you have to report of the people of the plain, Jared?"

Jared shuddered, this time not of cold. "Dark things, Bearer." He hesitated and looked around them, peering into the shadows. "They … they would have names."

Raphael was shocked. "That's impossible. It's nonsense."

"But still true."

"It isn't even meaningful. Are you mad?"

"They have broken the order of creation. They have remade themselves, and in remaking themselves, they become like men. They make themselves names and more."

"A body," Shet added. "A ka, a ba. A name to bind it all, and a shadow beneath."

"How do they do this?" Raphael was stunned. Even if what he was hearing was possible, it was outrageous. It overturned the order of things. It twisted Heaven's strictures.

"Hammering, at first. Brute force—rivets and sutures." Jared shuddered again and closed his eyes. "The howling in the caves turned my blood to ice to hear it. And then … something else. Azazel was the first."

"Of course he was," Raphael sneered.

"Something changed in him when he was through. Something that gave him power."

"What kind of power?"

"He has given it a name: *sorcery*. He makes new connections between things that were not tied, or he manipulates the bonds that do exist." Jared shook his head. "I don't think I can explain it any better than that. He *does* things."

"More sins? More rebellion?"

"I'm not sure. He uses it to change his followers."

"Do they all gain this thing, this *sorcery*?"

"I don't think so. He has befriended Mab. And he is building a city."

"To what end?" Raphael was puzzled. He had heard about the city already, though sorcery and the making of names were news to him. Still, the reminder of the city irked him. The outcast was not supposed to *do* anything, he was just supposed to be *gone*.

How dare he? Raphael wanted to ask, but Jared wouldn't have had any answer.

"I think the city *is* the end. It's huge, made of wood and stone and watered by canals. Many of our people flock to it."

"Why? What could the rebel possibly offer them?"

"They're calling it freedom," Jared said slowly. "I think it's something else. Maybe novelty? Maybe indulgence? Maybe belonging?"

Raphael wondered if a Writ would issue. He could only witness to the Chancellor what he knew; then he'd find out. "Well done," he said to the spy Jared. "Be sure to send word immediately of new developments."

"*Immediately* is difficult, Bearer. Too much absence is noted, so I can't just drop my tools and disappear on a whim."

"Take Enosh with you," Raphael said. "Send him back with word so you don't have to be absent."

Shet and Jared both nodded.

"May I have the honor of being your vessel on the return journey?" Shet asked, and Rafael condescended to nod.

Shet knelt to pray. Rafael exited his vessel Enosh.

CHAPTER FIVE

The good news was that he didn't have to cross the Mississippi. In the baronial anarchy into which the United States had fallen, a bridge over the mighty divide was a choking point too precious to leave unguarded.

He drove north and east through the night, slowly because he didn't want to turn on the Datsun's headlights. A fattening moon helped, snowing silver light upon the straight farm country highways and usually giving Raphael enough notice to avoid driving off the road when those highways took sudden right-angle jogs. The third time he skidded to a halt at the edge of a field of cornhusks, just after moonset, he decided it was enough. He coasted into a sheltered nook behind a stand of black walnuts, locked the Datsun's doors, and let himself sleep.

The morning's first ray of sun cracked straight across the frying-pan-flat field, blazed through the Datsun's windshield, and knocked open Enoch Emery's borrowed eyes. Raphael topped up the tank from the can, scarfed down an MRE—stroganoff, carrots, peaches, and a chocolate-coated graham cracker—and hit the road.

He followed the river without keeping it in sight, using Enoch's maps. Sterling looked too big on the map, so he made for Rock River at a highway bridge crossing, hoping it would be desolate.

It wasn't.

The men on the bridge didn't look like the barbarian warriors in the service of the Bull, though. They wore gray and green fatigues and they stood at attention, which seemed like marks of civilization to the tired Bearer of the Word. Even the green jeeps and the Humvee on the bridge behind them looked cheerful since they weren't burned to the ground or toppled over onto their sides.

They also held automatic rifles, and the Humvee had a machine gun mounted on top, which seemed … slightly less welcoming.

The foremost of the soldiers, a woman with graying hair tied into a bun behind her neck, raised a hand with her palm forward. Raphael stopped his car.

The woman walked around to Raphael's window as he cranked it down. "Sergeant Murdock," she said briskly. "Turn off your vehicle."

Raphael hesitated, but the sight of something that might have been a rocket launcher made up his mind. He wasn't going to get out of this by physical speed. He left the key in the ignition.

"Where am I?" he asked.

"Free State of Rock Island. What's your name, son?"

Son. Raphael smiled. "Enoch Emery." He looked again at the soldiers on and around the bridge and didn't see anything resembling the crude, animalistic banners that the Fallen had raised around their territories. He gestured at the mess inside the car. "I think I might even have ID somewhere in here, though I wasn't expecting to have to use it."

The Sergeant snorted, but her voice remained flat. "Ain't that the truth? I don't care about your ID, son, but this is a Free State toll bridge, and you're gonna have to pay the toll."

"Sure." He knew his wallet was empty, so Raphael dragged open the change drawer and started scooping quarters and nickels into his hand. "Does 'Free State' mean you don't serve the Bull?"

The woman leaned in closer, flashing blue eyes at Raphael. "We don't serve none of those goddamn monsters here, understood? No goddamn sorcerers, no goddamn fairies! We may not be U.S. Army anymore, but we're still human, by damn!"

Raphael nodded.

She leaned in closer still, and he could smell chewing tobacco on her breath. "How about you?" she asked.

"Am I human?"

"Do you serve the Bull?" she asked. "Or the Snake, or the Horse, or any of the rest of those … things?" She scanned the interior of the Datsun, and Raphael noticed that one hand rested on the butt of a semiautomatic pistol on her hip.

"No." That, Raphael thought, was the truth. Though he'd once been in uncomfortably close alliance with Belial, it hadn't lasted. He held the money up to the window, realizing it couldn't add up to more than a few dollars. "All I have are these coins."

Murdock knocked the coins to the ground. "Worthless shit! Copper, all of it, or worse! Maybe if the United States had made any *real* money, there'd still *be* a United States!"

"Okay." Raphael sighed. "Can I pay in kind? How about an MRE?" He shuffled among those that remained. "I can't read the name of the entree, but this one has raspberry cobbler for dessert."

"Not enough, Emery."

He heard the soft rasp of metal on leather behind him and knew that Sergeant Murdock had drawn her pistol. He kept his calm and smiled at her, not looking at the gun. "I could throw in a water bottle."

"You can throw in that gas can," she said. "And half the gas in your tank."

"I need the car. How about a flashlight?"

"I never said we'd take the *car*. Who'd want this piece of crap? Why don't you hand me the keys, and we'll make this quick?"

Raphael was no expert on mileage, but he was pretty sure the Datsun wouldn't make it to Minneapolis on half a tank of gas.

"Why don't you let me go without a payment instead?" he Whispered. "You'll be doing good. You'll be doing the right thing, the thing Heaven wants, the thing that will bring you back to the garden."

The warm winds of Eden blew into Sergeant Murdock's face. Harsh, deep lines of fatigue and rigor melted under the golden glow and the frankincense-spiked heat, and she smiled.

"Just tell your associates I've paid," he added, "and I'll be on my way."

Sergeant Murdock straightened up from the car with a smile on her face.

Raphael looked to the soldiers on the bridge and saw them adjust their aim as she stood.

They aimed at the Sergeant.

"Let him on through," she called, waving an arm. "He's paid!"

B-rap-p-p-p!

Three of the soldiers fired simultaneously, one short burst each, and then Isabella Murdock's body hit the asphalt.

Before they could turn their rifles on him, Raphael moved.

He sprang from the body of the vessel Enoch Emery, bursting through the Veil and upward like a klieg light. Enoch gasped and twisted as the Messenger emerged, floundering like a fish suddenly out of breath in the Datsun's front seat. Raphael didn't want the soldiers to shoot the man, or the car, so he rushed at them, into their midst and above them. They could shoot him, and the bullets would even hurt, but they wouldn't truly harm Raphael.

As he emerged, he saw the clawing hands of the damned, trying to drag themselves over the lip of the river's edge and failing.

Rat-tat-tat-tat-tat! Boom!

The men in fatigues fired. And missed.

Dear God, not another one. This one is on fire but at least it doesn't have an animal's head. Please, God, help me—

The Humvee driver was praying.

Perfect.

Raphael passed behind the Veil again and leaped into the driver. It was harder than entering Enoch, who not only prayed but prayed to invite the presence of a Messenger, but he forced his way through the soldier's battered and shaky name and deep into the connections among his parts.

"Where'd he go?" The question came from legs dangling at Raphael's shoulder, and he realized the gunner was asking.

"That way!" Raphael barked, and he put the Humvee in gear.

He slammed into one of the jeeps, knocking it through the railing at the side of the bridge and into the river. Men scattered and yelled, and he gunned the vehicle forward, slamming into each higher gear without taking his foot off the gas pedal.

"What the hell, Ramirez?" the gunner shouted.

"In those trees!"

Raphael barreled past the Datsun and off the road. Enoch lay crumpled on his side in the front seat, which was good. With luck, the soldiers would forget about him.

"I don't see it!" the gunner yelled back, but to be safe he let loose a volley of machine gun fire into the scraggly pines, sawing off limbs and sending up bursts of needles like the spray of sea foam. "Are you sure?"

Raphael checked his side mirror and saw soldiers following at a dead run. The surviving jeep also wheeled around and accelerated in his direction—

Past Sergeant Murdock's corpse and past the Datsun, which no one touched.

"Ramirez, you idiot, watch where you're going!"

Raphael focused on the ground ahead. Rocky earth skidded past in brownish sheets; the trees loomed immediately in front of him—

He threw the steering wheel to the right and exited the vessel Ramirez.

Abandoning two vessels in quick succession left him feeling drained, and the sudden all-squashing weight of the world didn't make him feel any better. Time seemed to slow as Raphael passed among the racing soldiers, hidden from their eyes by the Veil. A procession of damned men striking each other with bones paid him no more mind. Behind him, he heard the Humvee plow tumbling into the trees, the shouting of men, and more gunfire. He couldn't spare it any attention because of the weight bearing down on him.

If he'd had a body, he'd have been gasping.

Enoch sat up in the car and looked around wildly. Raphael passed the soldier's corpse and felt a shiver of pity.

She'd known she might die, he realized. Her own men had shot her, and it hadn't been an accident. It had been some sort of protocol, some plan. Her failure to exact a toll meant they'd shot her. Or maybe when she'd tried to wave him on she hadn't given some sort of countersign, and for that they'd shot her.

What was it she'd said? *Goddamn sorcerers and goddamn fairies?*

That was how the Free State of Rock Island had adapted to the broken world around them. Brutality, rigid rules, and the murder of their own.

Raphael trembled.

He let down the Veil, and Enoch saw him. The Son of Light immediately began to pray, and then Raphael was within him again, throwing the coupe into gear and racing forward across the Rock River.

He wanted to talk to Enoch, and he didn't quite know why. He was outraged. He felt guilt at Sergeant Murdock's death, maybe, and he wanted to tell someone what had happened and how it hadn't been his fault.

But even though he felt sick and weary inside Enoch, he felt worse outside. His kind had not really been created for the fallen world, he knew. He longed for Heaven, for Eden, for some sacred place where he could stand protected from the spiritual buffeting of the world and recover.

He wasn't going to find it in Minneapolis.

The Datsun bounced as its front tires jumped up onto the asphalt of the bridge. At the far side of the river, he checked his rearview mirror. The soldiers still fired shots in the woods, but no one was chasing him.

He was free.

* * *

Bearers of the Sword dragged the rebel Azazel away in chains. Shet's people had built a Stairway, the incense-and-light path down which Raphael and others had come to the assault, and the Swordbearers would take Azazel up that same route to be judged.

Raphael should have been following them, but he couldn't take his eyes off the City of Ainok.

It lay about him in smoking ruins. The great spiral-shaped canal was still, the sorcery that had fueled its flow broken, its waters dark with blood. Carnage darkened and clotted streets that had once been sparkling white.

They'd had it coming. They'd asked for it.

Azazel had been strangely submissive, though. Raphael frowned, trying to fathom the trick that must lie behind the docility. Maybe there was no trick. Maybe his had just been the weakness of the unrighteous.

He really should go. If the Stairway were dismantled, his only way to return to Heaven was if Heaven itself summoned him. But Shet's people would be in no hurry to take down the Stairway, he thought, and if they did, the Chancellor would surely recall Raphael. He was the hero of the Razing of Ainok, after all.

Raphael stood in a plaza beside a straight length of the canal, the wood and stone buildings surrounding him burning if they were not already collapsed. On the other side of the water stood Shet and a cadre of his men.

"Bearer!" Shet called to him. "Have you seen my son?"

Raphael shook his head. Enosh, once his vessel and a fellow Son of Light, had disappeared. Shet and his men marched under Heaven's banner in response to the Writ, but Shet also looked for his son.

"I'll search the ruins with you," Raphael answered.

Really, this was beneath Raphael's dignity, but he did it because he was a Son of Light. It still was not entirely clear to him what that meant at all times, but one thing it meant was that he helped other Sons whenever he could.

They fanned out.

Shattered mirrors everywhere. Their presence probably explained why so few of the trampled bodies on the ground belonged to the children of Mab. The fairies, mobile scraps and oddments left over from creation that they were, had escaped, and then someone had sealed the doors behind them. Had the fairies done that to prevent pursuit, or had Azazel's people broken the mirrors to protect Mab's children—or to cast them out?

Raphael moved towards the city center, drifting over the rubble. The thrill of the capture was past, and now he felt the weight of earth upon him again. The smoke around him was not the smoke of incense, not the pleasing smell of sacrifice creating the Stairway, but mere corruption.

He crossed a boulevard. Too many of the corpses were too mangled to be certain they weren't Enosh.

A figure rose from behind a freestanding wall ahead of him. The figure was Raphael's size and therefore not one of the children of men, despite its body of flesh and blood. Also, its head was the head of a serpent with the flared hood of a cobra.

"Corrupted thing!" Raphael snapped. "Have you no shame?"

The Fallen cringed, shuddering and hiding itself behind the wall.

"Archangel!" it hissed.

Raphael closed in on the abomination, and it cowered more but didn't flee. Finally it tossed aside a curved falchion and fell to its knees. Raphael inspected the monstrous thing. It was muscular and wore only a white kilt and sandals. If not for its grotesque reptile's head and its Messenger-like stature, it might have been a warrior of Shet's people.

"Why haven't you fled?" Raphael demanded. "Your blasphemous Prince is taken in chains and will not return. Your comrades are broken. Your inheritance was once the glory of Heaven, but now all that remains to you is the darkness of caves and the sightless worms of the pit."

Serpent Head held its hands up in supplication. "Don't you know me?" Its wrists were heavily scarred, as if something had gnawed on them. Like shackles. Or maybe the marks were burn scars.

Of course, the thing had once been a Messenger. Raphael stared at it, trying to see past the awkward cloak of meat that now hung on the once-angelic frame.

He shook his head slowly. "No. And I don't want you to tell me, either. Whatever you once were, you are no longer. You walked away from your home, and there can be no going back." He gestured with disdain at the Fallen's body. "Not like this."

The snake hissed, its shoulders shaking so hard it fell forward onto its hands and knees. Its hood retracted in misery.

Shet stepped into the boulevard a stone's throw away, where it debouched into a park, once green and now scorched black. He had two of his men with him, all three wrapped in breastplates and leading with the tips of their spears. "Enosh!" he called.

"You knew me!"

"Whatever I knew is gone." Raphael turned to go.

"I am still Kokhabel!" hissed the Fallen, weeping and making rattling noises in the back of its throat.

Raphael froze.

"Enosh!" Shet called again, before turning and marching into the burned park with his men.

Raphael pivoted back to the snake-headed Fallen who had once been Kokhabel, fellow Bearer of the Word—

And saw the scar.

It was a single long scar, and it ran all the way up the outside of one arm. He had seen it before.

"Enosh!" he heard Shet call again, far away.

"Enosh!" Raphael said. "You are the reason Shet's son didn't return to the tents of his people."

"Enosh was captured … I mean, *we* captured him."

Raphael looked again at the scars on Kokhabel's wrists. At the edges of one there remained a trace of bright blue ink—ink that Raphael himself had once applied to the young man's body.

"How?" he asked.

"These are not the ways of Heaven," Kokhabel sobbed. "You wouldn't understand."

"I can understand a thing and still hate it."

"Help me."

"I doubt there *is* help for you, you wretched *thing*."

"Bring me to the Chancellor. Bring me to the Hall of Fire. Let me beg for mercy." Kokhabel threw his arms around Raphael's body, and the Bearer of the Word felt that a mountain had fallen across him.

"There may be no mercy for you."

"Let me beg."

Raphael looked at Kokhabel and considered. "I can't," he said. "You're unclean. You stink of the ordure of flesh, of lust, of ambition, of anger, of lies. Such as you can't enter the halls of Heaven."

"The Writ," Kokhabel hissed, groveling even lower. Raphael looked back to the burned park and saw that Shet and his two men were coming back his way. "Let the Bearers of the Sword chain me and take me under the Writ. Even in chains before the Throne, one is still before the Throne."

"And one is still chained. But it doesn't matter, Kokhabel. The Writ is executed. It issued sealed from the Chancellor, it unbound the Bearers of the Sword, and what they came to do is done with the razing of Ainok and the capture of its Prince."

"Intercede, then." Kokhabel squeezed him tighter. "You are a Bearer of the Word. Bear my word to the Throne, to the Chancellor. Beg Heaven on my behalf. I'm penitent. I have erred, sinned grievously. Give me punishment, give me torment, cast me out, but let there be reconciliation and forgiveness one day. You are *God's healer*. Let there be healing."

Raphael snapped his wings with full force and jerked himself from Kokhabel's grasp. "You belong here," he said, looking around at the burning ruins. "This is what your ambition has wrought. You would not be patient, you would not do the will of Heaven, and instead chose your own will. Here they are, the fruits of your choice. May they be sweet to you."

"Please," Kokhabel said, one last time.

"I cannot." Raphael looked away.

"Enosh!" Shet and his two men advanced.

"What do I do?" Kokhabel asked the Bearer of the Word.

"You run."

The snake-headed Fallen sobbed and grabbed his sword from the bloodied white stones of the street. In his haste, he splashed over the boulevard's lip and into an arm of the canal, surging out of the bloody filth with his white kilt soiled and dark. Shet's two men raced after him, but with his large advantage of stride, they managed only to stab him in the heel as he fled. They chased still, howling with victory until the Fallen who had once been Kokhabel threw himself over the outer wall of Ainok and disappeared.

Shet leaned heavily on his spear and looked up at Raphael. "I think we will not find Enosh." He looked weary—as weary as Raphael felt.

"I think we will not," Raphael agreed. "I think you and your wife must perform the Rites of Comfort."

Shet nodded. "The hall of smoke and the Stairway will carry him before the Throne, I'm sure." He looked up at Raphael, and whatever he saw made him grin wryly. "As they must carry you, my friend. You've seen battle today and must rest. Allow me to offer myself as your vessel to take you back to my tent."

"Thank you."

Shet nodded again and began to pray.

*   *   *

Raphael couldn't tell when he passed into Wisconsin, but he thought it was probably somewhere in the middle of a vast swath of scorched earth, where the trees had been reduced to charred, upright toothpicks and the houses were nothing more than blackened concrete foundations. The burned zone took more than an hour to drive across.

He foraged where he could, finding a dozen sour green apples on a dying tree and a box of warm Otter Pops in a ditch beside a diner full of mangled skeletons. He tore the ends of the Pops off with his teeth and drank the colored sugar water inside, grateful for it but wishing he'd found gasoline and a hamburger instead.

The Wisconsin River was much easier to cross than the Rock River had been because the town of Boscobel was empty. Its buildings were gone too, reduced to matchsticks and torn shingles. At least the bridge still stood.

Raphael drove through the night, eating the last of the MREs to replenish his stores and the reserves of Enoch's body and ka. He saw Eau Claire as a reddish glow on the horizon and wondered who had set the city to the torch and why.

He crept into the periphery of the Twin Cities with his lights off, driving barely faster than a walking pace. Despite thick fog, Raphael could see and hear that the bridge over the St. Croix River was guarded, and under the banner of one of the Fallen—a banner the Bearer of the Word thought he knew. Men with spears and guns paced under burning torches. Lots of men.

He was so tired.

Raphael shut off the coupe to save gas and stared at white void that must be the river, frustrated.

It was so hard to travel like this, he thought. Maybe he should have come alone and never entered the vessel Enoch. Maybe he should leave Enoch now and go ahead without the young Son of Light. Of course, even if he did get across the St. Croix, he had no real way to locate Eddie Marlowe. He only knew that Eddie had declared that he would find the Skin of Adam and that the Daughters of Shet at the Nauvoo Pavilion had told him that last they knew, it had been on display in the Minneapolis Institute of Arts as a purported Algonquin artifact.

Maybe he never should have accepted to Bear this Word.

Maybe it was beyond him.

The shame Raphael felt at that thought burned Enoch's cheeks, and he kicked himself out of the Datsun. Acres of sprawling suburban homes stretched away to either side of the Freeway. He could chop up a table, he thought, and make a raft. No, that was insane. But he might find food and a place to sleep, and when he and Enoch both felt better, he might leave the vessel on this side of the river and go scout in Minneapolis. It would be tiring, but he could get across the St. Croix without having to fight or be seen.

Carefully shaping the beam of his flashlight with one hand, Raphael poked his head into the first home. He almost laughed with relief at what he saw.

Canoes.

They were staved in and useless, but he salvaged a paddle from the garage, which looked like a grenade had gone off inside it. But where one house had canoes, others should too. And they did.

He hid the car in a vacant lot behind a close row of tiny houses. In the soupy gray light preceding dawn, shivering from the chill despite a poncho he'd improvised from a wool blanket, Raphael dragged the canoe into the St. Croix River and hopped inside, paddling across underneath the bridge and the grinning, shimmering banner of the Serpent.

CHAPTER SIX

Raphael found a map of Minneapolis-St. Paul in a gas station whose windowpanes lay shattered about it in a glittering halo of shards. No food, but he drank rainwater collected in the twisted fragment of a rubber tire and kept going.

The Institute of Arts was on the map, so he headed for it as a cold rain began to fall. The shivering of Enoch's body and the rattling of his teeth made Raphael again consider simply leaving the vessel behind, but uncertainty about what lay ahead stopped him.

Enoch seemed dedicated, and he had a gun. A pistol was a clumsy and inelegant thing, but it solved some problems that could be intractable to the Whisper of Eden.

He moved slowly, cutting through yards and wooded parks whenever he could. Away from the highways and in the outskirts, the signs of human life were few and far between. Deer grazed on lawns that had been regularly mowed as recently as this summer. Raphael wasn't surprised to see mangy, neglected-looking cats and dogs chasing after small prey through overturned garbage cans and down cracking asphalt streets, but the otters and badgers caught him off guard. Raphael shooed a trio of otters away from one dumpster and recovered a thick plastic garbage bag, the kind that's two millimeters thick so you can stuff it with tree trimmings. There was already a convenient hole in the bottom, so Raphael stuck his head through it and wore the bag like a poncho.

As the day wore on, he trudged closer to the center of the Twin Cities and began to see more people. Whatever exactly had wasted or driven away much of the population of the sprawling, semi-urban metropolis, the survivors had responded by pulling into the center of the city and posting guards on all the bridges.

In the afternoon, the rain broke. Stooping to enter a tennis court through a gash in the chain-link fence surrounding it, Raphael heard a voice.

"You aren't one of us, are you?"

He stepped onto the green surface and straightened up. Three men faced him, one holding a sawed-off shotgun and the others wearing machetes very prominently on their belts. Shotgun wore a fleece jacket and had tattoos on the temples of his gray, scaly face. Raphael had to squint before he could make out that the tattooed images were serpent fangs, and when he saw them, he realized that Shotgun's eyes were too far apart and too beady to be truly human.

One of Shotgun's companions was dressed in a green—and-brown serape with a cobra stitched into its wool in gold thread, and the other wore a green parka whose gray, fur-lined hood entirely hid its owner's face. Raphael couldn't be sure, but he thought he heard soft weeping from the void inside the fur.

"Shut up!" Shotgun hissed, and punched Parka in the arm. Parka shuffled sideways with the force of the blow, and Raphael saw that he was wearing snakeskin boots.

The people of Minneapolis-St. Paul are the tribe of the snake now, Raphael thought.

Kokhabel.

Raphael considered what to say and kept his hands away from the pistol in the back of his belt.

"Tell us who you are, then," Serape said, the wool of his garment trembling slightly to his Minnesota twang. He was a thin man with a few wiry hairs clinging to his skull and the shriveled lips of someone who'd lost a lot of teeth, though he didn't look old. He put his hand on the handle of his machete. He smiled, and Raphael saw what was wrong with his gums— all his teeth had fallen out but for a pair of fangs revealed by his curling upper lip.

Clearly, Raphael was going to need to change his appearance if he wanted to fit in.

Or rather, since being a snake was the issue, he was going to have to change his skin.

"I am a refugee and a stranger here," he Whispered. The warm winds that blew through him were particularly welcome given the weather, and the frankincense masked the sour tang of the men's bodies. "I need your coat and whatever food and water you can give me."

He hesitated while the men struggled, the face of each slowly collapsing into placid, peaceful surrender.

"Also, I need your weapons."

* * *

Raphael swallowed the last of the beef jerky with the last swing of water from a tin bottle.

At least, he hoped it was beef jerky. Or something innocuous, like dog.

He pushed the bottle into the knotted garbage bag that had earlier been his poncho, careful not to drop it so it wouldn't clink against the shotgun or the two machetes. He wore his newly acquired green parka, hood down so he could see and hear, though that left his face exposed. Also, the memory of Parka's forked tongue slithering dully over leathery lips when the man had removed the coat made Raphael less than eager to wrap his face in the same gray fur lining. He'd moved Enoch Emery's .357 to a hip pocket of the winter coat and tried to keep one hand within easy reach of the pocket at all times. Not that he was much of a shot.

Doom, doom, da-doom, thundered the drums outside.

Raphael lingered inside the blasted lobby of some kind of church. What kind he couldn't tell, since rain and barbarism had torn away any writing he might once have been able to see. But the crowd outside, the drummers and the dancers and the ones who just looked stoned, avoided the church. Probably not because it was hallowed ground, though that might be it. Maybe they were just superstitious.

Raphael crouched in the church's lobby. Darker than the shadows that enveloped him gaped a double doorway leading into what was presumably the church's meeting hall. Two hallways wandered off at right angles from each other in the gloom towards the far corners of the building. Battered metal folding chairs and pulpy, mildewing hymnals, their pages clumped together and rotting, lay across the lobby's floor in front of Raphael like flowers strewn before a bride.

Across the street over which Raphael gazed was a park. Washburn Fair Oaks Park, the map called it. It wasn't much, just a flat green space and some trees. Now it looked like something out of ancient Tyre; the rain had stopped, the clouds had eased up without disappearing, and in the last chill rays of an aloof sun, the park was filled with worshippers.

They were naked, and the night's darkness wasn't going to hide their brazenness. As the sky streaked orange over the leafless trees, the people began to light torches.

Only they weren't people. Not quite. Not anymore.

Raphael sighed and turned away, trying not to look at the scales, the missing arms replaced with snapping serpents, the webbed and taloned lizards' feet at the bottom of shapely women's legs.

Kokhabel. How had he gone so wrong?

Did he love his cursed Fallen form so much, he shared it as a blessing with his followers?

Doom, doom, da-doom.

Raphael ignored the crowd as it began to writhe and sin. He looked over their heads at the Institute of Arts.

The facade of the building facing the park had the pillared Greek look that Americans used when they wanted to convince each other that the things going on inside a building were holy and important—it looked like Congress or a bank. A wooden scaffold had been erected on its steps so that from the front doors of the Institute one could walk out along a level gangplank and stand at the top of a tower facing the park.

Beneath the wooden tower was piled a huge clutter of objects Raphael couldn't quite make out.

Some of the crowd—those not already stoned or descending into lascivious frenzy—brought armfuls of wood and shoved them under the base of the tower. He finally saw the drums; a row of great, skin-covered monstrosities squatted at the base of the Institute's steps.

This was where Eddie Marlowe and the shreds of his rock-and-roll band had been headed, to steal the Skin of Adam. They thought the Skin might heal their companion Twitch Pony, the child of Mab.

They might be right.

The price Adam had paid for the Skin, though, was to be driven out of Eden. Raphael wondered what price the fairy Twitch would pay.

It was no surprise the Skin had ended up here. Many ancient items of power had been destroyed in their time or in the eons since, but those that had survived or had been rediscovered found themselves in an era that did not believe in them. They were no longer weapons, shields, boons, bridges, or elixirs; they were souvenirs. They ended up in universities, in private collections, in museums. Sometimes, having been utterly misidentified, they simply ended up in junk heaps.

Raphael wondered how he was going to find out whether Marlowe had been here, whether he had found the Skin, and where he might be now. He sighed, luxuriating in the purely human sensation of calm resignation that came with air hissing from his borrowed lungs. In the morning, he thought. The orgy would leave a wreckage of stunned and dazed cultists in its wake. He'd go among them and ask them questions when they were at their most stupid.

Eddie Marlowe might not stand out, but these revelers should remember the Marked Woman and the broken fairy.

The moment Raphael turned to slip back into the darkening church, something lurched into the corner of his vision. It was huge and moving erratically, and at the first, not-quite-comprehending glimpse of it, Raphael fell to the cold, damp industrial carpet squares on the church's floor.

He jammed his fist into the parka pocket and ripped out the pistol.

Kicking himself back to his feet and against the rough brick of one wall, he knocked one booted foot against a folding chair, sending it sliding across the floor with a loud *dong*.

Doom, doom, da-doom.

Raphael froze, fearing that the chair's noise had been heard outside. He pressed himself against the wall, getting behind the doorframe, blinding himself to what happened outside in order to keep himself out of sight.

In the old days, Bearing the Word had never been this tricky.

Shrieks of ecstasy and hunger outside told him he hadn't been heard, and he slipped his head into the doorway to get a look at … a ship.

Not a ship, but a bark. Flat, rough-hewn, vast. Curling up fore and aft, with banks of rowers reaching out into the crowd with oars. Some of the shrieking, Raphael saw, came from the crowd. The oars weren't simply wooden paddles but blades, and as worshippers rushed forward, they were cut and mauled. Human appendages and severed serpentine things flew through the air and flailed indiscriminately in the crowd.

A blue sail hung slack from a high crossbeam, and the bark moved forward on rollers. Dozens—no, hundreds, Raphael realized as he got a better look over the moist, sweating heads of the crowd—of men and women strained at thick cables, all knotted into a brass ring at the bark's prow. Among the humans pulling were horses, big draft animals with cables wrapped around their necks or knotted to their harnesses. Logs as thick around as two men standing shoulder to shoulder thundered and groaned beneath the flat bottom of the bark, and as each tumbled out behind the moving vessel, Kokhabel's worshippers seized it, dragged it with dozens of arms to the side, and rushed it forward to throw it in front of the bark again, at the heels of the cable-pullers.

Thousands of people pulled, heaved, hoisted, and pushed, and the bark moved forward. The sheer effort was something Raphael hadn't seen in centuries, not since the invention of the combustion engine and modern construction techniques. Watching the bark moving was like watching the construction of the pyramids.

He hated to admit it, but the bark's central occupant only added to the spectacle. Kokhabel sat cross-legged in the middle of the bark, which was barely wide enough to hold him. He sat on something that might have been folded sheets of cloth or reed mats, just before the sail. He was bare chested, as always. His snakelike head swung slowly left and right, tongue flickering in and out, scenting the musk, sweat, and fear of the crowd. The eyes, beaded and whiteless, rested on everyone and on no one.

The eyes seemed to rest on Raphael.

Doom, doom, da-doom.

Raphael shrank back and cocked the pistol.

In response to the gun's *click*, he heard a shuffling in the darkness behind him.

He spun around, jamming himself against the brick wall and stabbing at the gloom with the barrel of the .357.

"*Hijo de putas*, gun down!" snapped a shadow's voice.

Raphael blinked. "I know you." He didn't lower the pistol.

The other man stepped closer, moving his face from the lobby's darkness into a pool of ruddy yellow torchlight. He held a pistol too, and pointed it squarely at Raphael. He did look familiar, but it took Raphael a moment to figure out why and recognize him.

He'd lost a lot of weight.

"The bass player," Raphael said. "You're Mike."

The rock and roller cocked his head and squinted. He still wore the cracked brown leather jacket Raphael had first seen on him in New Mexico, but it was much dirtier now, and it hung off his body like a scarecrow's coat. The tangle of superstition on his breast—a cross, a rabbit's foot, other things Raphael couldn't distinguish—hung in a hollow cave made by his now-sunken chest. Mike looked half his size.

"Do I know you?"

"Dudael, New Mexico," Raphael reminded him. "You found me hiding inside the synagogue's geniza. Only, of course, I was deceiving you." He felt a little proud of himself at the memory, but then realized he didn't really want to snub Mike. Not when the bass player had a .45 pointed at him. "Not that I fooled you for long," he added.

Mike spat on the ground. "Huh."

Was he mistaken? Raphael lowered his pistol slowly and put it back in the pocket of his parka. It was a sign of goodwill. "You're Mike, aren't you?"

Mike's face spasmed, and his shoulders twitched. He jerked backwards in an awkward step that looked like he was dancing, or wrestling with an invisible opponent.

Raphael frowned.

"*¡Maricón que seas!*" Mike snapped. He jammed his gun into the back of his pants and threw himself to the floor. Grunting, he planted his knuckles in the cold carpet and began doing push-ups, over and over.

Doom, doom, da-doom.

Had the bass player lost his mind? Raphael didn't care as long as the man knew where to find the rest of the band. "This is a strange time to exercise."

Mike bobbed in and out of the pool of murk about the floor several times before lurching to his feet. "Yeah," he huffed, "but Mike needed to be taught a lesson."

Mike? "What lesson?"

"That I'm in charge, *chucha.*" The bass player drew his gun again and pointed it at Raphael. His breath came in ragged pants, and in the yellow light of torches that filtered in from the Washburn Fair Oaks Park, his dark eyes glittered, beady and malicious. "Now where were we?"

"Who are you?" Raphael hissed. He felt like screaming, but the crowd outside suddenly seemed closer—in the same room, even—and he couldn't attract attention.

"That's a good damn question, but it ain't the one I care about. What do you want from my brother?"

"Your brother?"

"Mike, you *chupacabra*. Don't waste your time telling me you're an old school friend and it's a coincidence running into each other like this. That's bullshit; leave it at home. You're looking for Mike. Why?"

"I'm looking for Eddie."

Mike—or whoever this was that looked like Mike—laughed, dry and hollow. "That's funny."

Raphael felt disquieted. "I didn't mean it as a joke. Where's Mike?"

"It doesn't matter what you *meant* as a joke, does it? Everything's a joke. All of it." Mike waved his gun around. "Life, death, heaven, hell. That crazy shit outside, the guy with the snake head. It's all a joke because they tell you it matters, they tell you there's right and wrong and consequences; you go to heaven if you're good and hell if you're bad, but they're wrong. It doesn't matter what you do. Nobody goes to heaven. That's the joke. Maybe there is no heaven after all. There's pointless life, and then there's hell. And hell is like country music. It goes on forever, and you can't shut it out."

"And Mike?"

"Mike's right here."

Raphael considered. The pistol in his pocket felt heavy, dragging down one side of his parka. "Who am I talking to? You're Mike's brother, but what's your name?"

The man considered, then lowered his gun slightly. Now the pistol only pointed at Raphael's knees. "Chuy. You?"

Raphael nodded. "Raphael. You look just like your brother. Where's Mike, Chuy?"

Chuy chuckled softly and tapped the muzzle of his pistol against his own temple. "You ain't listening." He tapped the gun against his head again. "He's right here."

Raphael hesitated. Was this possession or madness? "Can I talk to Mike?"

"You wouldn't want to. He's chickenshit, and an idiot. Besides, you don't need him. If you're looking for Eddie Marlowe, I can tell you where he is."

"Oh yeah?"

Chuy pointed out the door into the park. "He's the guy with the tambourine."

Raphael looked.

He saw now that he'd been distracted by the size of the boat, by the crowd, and by the presence of Kokhabel, and that he'd missed the other occupants of the bark. Four men, two in front of Kokhabel and two behind, stood at the corners of the bark with hooked knives in their hands. Their heads were shaved, and their robes, once white, were darkened with blood. From unseen sources at their feet, behind the bark's rowers, the men with knives pulled a steady succession of sheep, chicken, cats, dogs, and other creatures, holding each up in turn before dispatching it with a single slice of the knife and tossing its carcass to the crowd. As the cultists around the boat snatched at the dismembered animals, they in turn were dismembered by the relentless bladed oars of the bark.

Kokhabel's hands rested on his knees, and Raphael now saw that the Fallen's hands weren't empty. The hand farther away from Raphael held a person—the darkness and the various things obscuring his view left Raphael uncertain, but from the curly black hair on the captive's head, it could be the Marked Woman. The near hand held the silver-haired fairy Twitch, who flopped like a fish on a riverbank, twitching and spineless.

In the front of the bark stood Eddie Marlowe. He glared over his shoulder at Kokhabel with a fierceness that would cut stone, but he stood still. Raphael couldn't tell whether the guitar player's ankles were shackled or tied to something, but in each hand, the man held a tambourine.

Doom, doom, da-doom.

The bark rumbled towards the front steps of the Institute and the wooden tower resting on the jumble of artifacts. Raphael pressed himself closer into the doorway to see better and realized there was another element of the scene he had missed. He saw it first as streaks of shadow zipping through the air between him and the torches, but when he heard hissing sounds from the sidewalk, he realized what it was.

Snakes. Snakes in the grass and the street, snakes whipping through the air on Infernal wings.

To a signal Raphael hadn't heard, three enormous bonfires sprang into life, two in the park and the third in the street that had once separated the park from the Institute, back when there had been automobile traffic. Kokhabel and his bark, including the rock-and-roll band prisoners, instantly became silhouettes.

"Play," Kokhabel rasped.

Eddie Marlowe raised the tambourines.

CHAPTER SEVEN

Raphael crossed the lobby quickly, from the watery darkness opening onto the street in front into a near-black, cryptlike gloom. Just inside the doors, a shattered bench lay across his path. Enoch's Heaven-filled muscles made short work of it, heaving the wood and upholstery out of the way without effort. He tossed the garbage bag with its shotgun and two machetes to the floor.

"Hey." Chuy's objection sounded pro forma, but he didn't shoot, didn't even raise the pistol again, and when Raphael moved into the next room, he followed.

Raphael stopped in the center and looked over the interior of the church's meeting hall. No windows. The double doors on the other side of the room were shut. Seeing through Enoch's eyes in the darkness, he could barely see at all. The front of the hall was choked with wreckage of some kind, and upended pews lay strewn about the room like so many pick-up sticks.

"What are you doing?" Chuy asked.

Raphael turned and saw the other man silhouetted in the doorway. "Come in or go out," he said. "Either way, I close the door now. I have to plan."

"Why you gotta close the door?" Chuy asked, but he stepped inside and pulled the door most of the way shut with one hand.

Darkness descended, but it didn't escape Raphael's notice that the bass player's body with his brother's soul apparently inside kept the pistol in his other hand. At least he kept it pointed at the floor. "You gonna plan naked or something?"

"Yes," Raphael said, and he exited Enoch Emery's body.

Chuy spat out a stream of quick, emphatic Spanish that Raphael didn't recognize, and raised his gun. Raphael saw him clearly now because Raphael's own powers of vision weren't dependent on the light visible to humans, and also because the white light of Raphael's own presence sprayed the interior of the meeting hall with glory.

The weight of the world crushed down on Raphael. Without Enoch's body, he felt tired and weak. Still, he drifted slightly up into the air, letting the light of his being settle on the darkness of the church hall like snow on a Christmas morning.

Enoch crumpled to the floor.

"Wait," Raphael Whispered, raising a hand to stay Chuy.

He saw Chuy now, distinct from Mike, just as he saw the damned punishing each other on the surface of the earth. Mike's body held them both. Mike's ba looked pudgier and shabbier than his body now was, but Chuy's was lean, fierce, tattooed, and bleeding from numerous wounds. They locked with each other in something that might have been an intimate embrace or the first step of a wrestling throw, both scowling.

They looked up at Raphael and stopped, still aiming the gun. It seemed to be a point that united them.

That was fine, of course. Getting shot would be painful, but it wouldn't injure him, and as long as they were aiming at Raphael, they weren't aiming at Enoch.

He didn't see any of the damned, though. Curious, Raphael looked around. The interior of the church had been wrecked by flooding and maybe by theft. The large wooden cross that was supposed to hang centered on the wall in front of the congergation had slipped and now leaned against the wall to the left, its peak and one arm grinding out two dusty craters in the pulverized brick. The fallen cross had reduced the church's electric organ to toothpicks and wire, but the cross was in one piece, and there were no damned in the room.

No damned and no snakes. *Consecrated ground.* Raphael hadn't been on consecrated ground since he'd left Dudael, and something about the notion that a believing holy man had prayed over this room and for its protection cheered him up a little. It felt a little bit like coming home.

Such a prayer probably wouldn't stop Kokhabel—though that might depend on the holy man in question—but it looked like it was holding back some of the Fallen's minions.

"*Chucha*," Chuy groaned. "You're one of them."

"Fear not," Raphael said. "And don't shoot. We don't want to attract any attention."

Chuy looked like he was having no problem following the instruction not to fear. He looked belligerent. "Who are you?"

"You can call me Raphael. I am a Bearer of the Word." Ba-Mike spasmed within the prison of his own body, but Ba-Chuy held him back.

"Yeah?" Chuy asked. "What do you want from me, Raphael?"

"Your help. I need to get to Eddie Marlowe."

Chuy laughed. Finally, he shoved the pistol into his jacket pocket. "Getting to him is easy. You just run out there fast enough to avoid getting killed. Then what?"

Raphael didn't know. He could rush out and reach Eddie, of course. He could simply drift out, obscured by the Veil, and reveal himself to Bear the Word at the last possible second. But Chuy was right—then what? It would do Heaven little good to have a called prophet who was then immediately hacked to pieces by frenzied, orgiastic followers of the Fallen Kokhabel.

Too bad. If the outcome Heaven wanted was impossible, Heaven would have to settle for what could be achieved.

"Maybe 'then nothing,'" he admitted.

"Is that what they sent you for?"

"Heaven can be surprisingly inscrutable. Even to its own."

"Don't seem right."

Ba-Mike whipped suddenly sideways, throwing his arms around Ba-Chuy's neck. Their shared body staggered backwards with a loud "Oomph," and then Chuy threw himself to the floor and started doing push-ups again.

Raphael had to agree; it didn't seem right.

Enoch groaned and rolled up onto his knees, pointing at Chuy, who frenetically pumped up and down on the meeting hall floor. "Who's that?" the Son of Light croaked.

"A companion of Eddie Marlowe's," Raphael told him.

Chuy charged to his feet, breathing hard. Enoch stood warily.

"Impressive pushups," Enoch said, "but I gotta ask, what the hell are you doing?"

"Son of a bitch hates it," Chuy sneered. "All that slob wants to do is get drunk, eat candy bars, and pretend he likes girls."

"Yeah? Who's that, then?"

Chuy looked to Raphael and back to the vessel. "Son of a bitch inside me," he said. "Though it looks like you might know exactly what I'm talking about. Son of a bitch my brother. Son of a bitch who killed me and damned me to Hell because he was so desperate to prove he was attracted to women."

Enoch shook his head. "I don't know your brother. Sounds like you two had a rough time."

"Rough time? I had nothing all my life," Chuy spat. "I got even less now, and that son of a bitch is to blame."

"You made bad choices," Raphael said, and immediately wished he hadn't.

"You think it's that easy?" Chuy laughed. "Everybody makes bad choices. *Everybody!* Except you, I guess. Guess that's why you get to be all glowing and fifty feet tall. 'Cause you're perfect—you never made a wrong call, not since the day the Horseshoe Crab Nebula crapped you out along with all the other glowing white turds."

Raphael felt uncomfortable and said nothing.

Chuy stared the angel in the eye. "Too right, bitch," he said. "I saw you down there in Hell. I guess you must not have noticed me, but I saw you, and guess what, Silver Surfer? You were on the *wrong damn side*! It was you and that octopus devil and the fairy queen and the wizard and all the giant flies, wasn't it?"

"I wasn't fighting Heaven." It was a lie, and Raphael knew it. "Both sides were wrong in that struggle."

Enoch looked away, as if politely avoiding an awkward conversation.

Chuy laughed again, ignoring the falsehood. "Here's the thing: the whole world's gone to Hell now, and the only guy who's been willing to take a chance on me has been Eddie Marlowe. Eddie and that crazy black girl, Qayna."

"What about your brother?" Raphael asked. "Maybe it's his fault you died, but you're in his body somehow. I don't know how you're doing it, but I know enough about the structure of the human essence to think he must be somehow permitting you."

Chuy jerked spastically and ground his teeth hard. "Even with … whatever happened with Mike," he managed to squeeze out, "I was stuck. Eddie and the Marked Woman, they dragged me out."

Raphael could only nod.

"Where I stand," Chuy continued, "I see two options. I run away like an animal and die like an animal, cold, starving, and alone. Or I stay and fight like a man."

"You may die like a man," Enoch said soberly.

"So be it." Chuy drew his pistol. "You're here to see Eddie Marlowe? I'm with you. Let's spring him."

"I'm with you too," Enoch told Raphael. "You know I've already been anointed for my burial."

"I know." Raphael considered.

"We'd better hurry, though," Chuy said. "I think Captain Snake Head wants to sacrifice Eddie on that pile of museum junk. I can tell you from experience, that kind of shit will really ruin your day."

Enoch looked up to Raphael. "What museum junk?"

"I didn't see clearly."

"I didn't either," Chuy threw in, "but the Skin of Adam was definitely in the pile—Qayna recognized it—along with a whole bunch of other stuff. Swords and spears, armor, old writings, and some statues, amulets, and charms. What do you think they're doing out there? It isn't the office Christmas party, *mijito*. They mean business."

"We don't need the Skin," Raphael decided. It was clearly true—he had been sent to Bear the Word to Eddie Marlowe, so the health of the fairy Twitch was beside the point. "Much less the other stuff. Unless the Sword of Goliath is in the pile; that might come in handy."

"Yeah, but—"

"We don't need the Skin of Adam." Raphael drew himself up straight and Whispered. He'd had enough argument. "Do we?"

"No ..." Chuy said slowly into the warm frankincense wind. He dragged out and broke the single syllable like it cost him an internal struggle just to pronounce it.

"Why?" Enoch asked.

"I'm here to Bear the Word," Raphael said gently, "not to right every wrong in the world. That's an infinite task, a bottomless well of sorrow, and even Heaven doesn't attempt it. It's impossible." Besides, it was someone else's task, not his. He was a Bearer of the Word, not a healer of fairies. If the Sisters of Nauvoo could do nothing for Twitch, perhaps it was best that others stopped trying.

"Heaven doesn't attempt it, or Heaven fails?" Enoch asked. It was a very direct question for a Son of Light, and expressed surprising uncertainty. Raphael had to remind himself that Enoch Emery was a recent initiate.

"Mostly, Heaven leaves you to your own devices," Raphael said. "You're supposed to do the righting of wrongs." As he said it, he wondered who he was talking to, and he was grateful he didn't have the ability to blush. "You humans, I mean."

"I see. But I meant, why does the Serpent want to sacrifice anyone on top of the museum's artifacts?" Enoch said. "There would be easier ways to kill Marlowe. Bite him, for starters, or simply step on him."

"Snake Head's got a grudge against Eddie," Chuy said. His dazed look was fading, but he still had a placid expression on his face. "Wants him to die special. Something to do with something that happened back in Oklahoma. I guess Eddie got in his way."

"That explains the sacrifice," Enoch admitted, "but not the artifacts.

"Blood is life and power," Raphael said. "I don't understand it fully, and maybe no one does, or maybe these are simply mysteries above my degree. But blood has something to do with the connection among a person's ba, ka, and body. A person's blood and his name are, somehow, the same thing."

"You don't have blood," Chuy guessed, skeptical.

"I don't have any of those things," Raphael agreed. "I am *simple*, and I simply *am*. But Eddie Marlowe has blood and a name."

"You have a name," Chuy objected. "You just told me. It's Raphael."

"That's not a name." Raphael tried to be patient. "That's only a label. A name is something else. A name is your identity, the thing you are, the power that binds together all your parts."

"All the parts you don't have." Chuy looked skeptical.

"You should understand this. You don't have all your parts either, right now."

"What are you talking about? I got a body and a spirit."

"You're borrowing someone else's body," Raphael contradicted him. He looked closer at the brothers knitted together. "I'm not sure about your name—I can't see how you're joined, but maybe you have the same name. I'm guessing you're borrowing Mike's ka, too. Your shadow is a complete mess. Really, you two are a tangled mess together, and your combined shadow simply shows it."

Chuy cocked his head to one side and then snorted. "Was that a slam?"

"It was if the truth hurts you."

Chuy gestured vaguely at Enoch Emery and frowned. "Is that what you do? Borrow his body and his ... ka? His name?"

Something flickered in Chuy's eyes. It might have been hope.

So Chuy didn't like the fact that he was bound to his brother. He wanted out.

"I'm not the same as you," Raphael pointed out. "I am simple—a point, a tiny thing of the spirit. Among the five parts of a human being there is infinitely more space than I need to be comfortable. I was made to do this; you are a different order of creature. I enter through a man's name, through his blood, and I rest inside of him."

Enoch laughed dryly. "Funny how it doesn't really seem like *rest* to me."

Raphael continued, "You and your brother are bound somehow. I do not understand it." He considered. "It feels wrong to me. Not Infernal, not rebellious, but ... broken. Your bond feels to me like the presence of the damned on the surface of the Earth."

"It *is* the presence of the damned on the surface of the Earth," Chuy granted. "Me and Mike, that's both of us—damned."

"Don't be so sure," Enoch warned.

"So what do you do?" Chuy pressed. "Come out through the name or the blood? Do you say the person's name or something?"

"A person's name isn't the simple label by which you call him on the street," Raphael said, feeling slightly irritable for the fact that he was wasting his time arguing with this broken person. "I have a label, too—*Raphael*. A *name* is something different. Most mortals don't know their own names, and usually wouldn't be able to pronounce the name if they even did know it."

"What do you do, then? Just ... exit?"

"It is my nature," Raphael agreed. "I am a Bearer of the Word."

Chuy looked disappointed, but the wheels of his brain continued to grind. "So the blood over all the museum junk is ... what? To give the stuff a name?"

"Yes," Raphael said. "Or to give it power, which is the same thing. To render it active. To turn it on, light it up."

"Religion," Chuy snorted. "All this weird talk of blood and names reminds me why I stopped going to Mass."

"Who said anything about *religion*?" Raphael asked with a smile. "We were talking about *power*."

"What about going into Eddie's body?" Chuy suggested.

"Can you Bear the Word to him inside his own body?" Enoch was skeptical.

"I can't," Raphael agreed. "But in any case, the goal is to free him. I might be able to enter him if he happened to be praying—though Eddie doesn't seem like the type. But then what? I'd be chained and surrounded." He hesitated. "I'll need your help."

"I'm a Son of Light."

Chuy just nodded. "Just make it quick, Rafi. We're running out of time."

"I'll distract Kokhabel."

"Kokhabel?" Chuy scratched his head.

"Snake Head. I'll distract him, and I think it's safe to say I can probably distract all of them."

"That's good," Chuy said. "I don't always have a plan, but when I do, I like it to include a distraction."

"While I'm distracting them, you need to free Eddie Marlowe."

"And what, just walk out?" Chuy's face was incredulous. "Aren't you forgetting he's surrounded?"

"If I had a helicopter, I'd give it to you." Raphael tried not to snap in reply.

"There are horses." Enoch's voice was so calm and quiet, Raphael almost didn't hear him.

"Maybe *you* know how to ride a horse, *maricón*. Where I grew up, a kid was lucky to have a *skateboard*. And if you hadn't figured it out yet, I wasn't one of the lucky ones."

"I know how to ride a horse," Enoch agreed. He took his pistol from his parka pocket and handed it grip-first to Chuy. "You know how to shoot a gun."

"There's a shotgun in that bag," Raphael added. "And machetes, if it comes to that."

Chuy looked from Enoch to Raphael and back again. His expression was skeptical, but he took the pistol and held it in a firm grip. There was a hint of a wild laugh in his voice when he spoke. "I could shoot you both now."

Enoch Emery shrugged with a wry grin. "Shooting him would be pointless," he said, "and I'm prepared to die for the Light."

Chuy shook his head. "You guys are crazy."

Enoch smiled even wider. "We're not crazy," he said. "We're *believers*."

"That's nothing special," Chuy guffawed. "Hell is full of believers."

Enoch ignored him and turned instead to Raphael. "What's the order?" he asked.

Raphael nodded; there was no time for theology now. "You two get into position. Enoch, by the horses. Chuy, at a right angle from Eddie's location, beyond the crowd, so you can give Enoch and Eddie covering fire when they make a break for it. I'll ... disappear, and when I reappear, I'll be behind Kokhabel—Snake Head. They'll turn around, and that's your signal to move."

"And the Skin of Adam?" Enoch asked.

"And the fairy? And Qayna?" Chuy added.

"Our mission," Raphael reminded them both, "is just Eddie Marlowe."

He slipped behind the Veil.

Chapter Eight

aphael slipped into the church's lobby through the cracked doors and then drifted out onto the park, all under the concealment of the Veil.

Kokhabel's bark approached the stone steps beneath the Institute's facade. The drums of this perverse worship, which had been muted while Raphael had been inside the meeting hall, boomed loud and fast. *Doom, doom, da-doom*, and underneath it raced a shimmering silver-brass aural glow that had to be Eddie Marlowe on the tambourine.

Kokhabel's misbegotten worshippers flailed about in the park, in the street, and on the steps. Darkness mercifully concealed much of what they did, though not their nudity. Those far away from the bonfires seemed impervious to the cold, and those too close to the scorching heat seemed immune to the roasting power of the flames. A wild, wavering ululation filled the air such as Raphael hadn't heard in centuries. A steady *hiss* ran through all the noise like the sound of a thousand snakes, and Raphael saw that far more of the worshippers than he had previously realized had snake parts for arms, legs, or for a head. Lizards slithered among them, heaping themselves near the fires for their warmth. A carpet of snakes writhed and wriggled all over the park, and a storm of them darted through the air like a cloud of mosquitoes in a swamp.

On the wooden tower over the Institute's steps stood three more men with shaved heads and white robes, and Raphael now saw a line of captives being led up the tower's ramp. They were naked—men, women, and children—and they were roped neck to neck to neck.

As the draft horses rumbled closer, two of the shaved men led the first captive out along the ramp to the tower. Rising and drifting to position himself behind the bark, Raphael saw that a block of wood sitting on the tower was hacked into the rough shape of a coiled and self-devouring serpent. It was an altar, and Kokhabel's sorcerers led the prisoner forward to it, where their third comrade waited with a long, hooked knife in his hand. A cloud of darting serpentine flesh hung over the crowd.

The boy was blond haired and had a fox-shaped face. He looked like a younger version of Enoch Emery.

It was time to act.

Directly behind Kokhabel's bark and drifting above the ground, Raphael let the Veil drop. It was his imagination, he knew, but the weight of the world felt even heavier outside the Veil. The writhing bodies below—human, serpentine, and other—half-concealed and half-revealed by the erratic orange light of the bonfires, either didn't see him or ignored him. That was fine.

Doom, doom, da-doom.

He could fix that.

Every Bearer of the Word had three gifts of communication that defined his nature and role. First, he could Bear the Word Itself—no other class of Messenger, no other agent of Heaven, Earth, or Hell was capable of doing so, and a Bearer of the Word could only do it by commission. The Word chose the Bearer rather than the other way around. A Bearer had more control over the Whisper of Eden, which he used when he chose and which could not be resisted—or at least, was difficult for those who were descended from Adam and Eve to resist. Eden poisoned them the same way oxygen did—they would die without it, or at least without some idea and hope of it, and they would die for it.

Every Bearer of the Word could also speak at will with the Still Small Voice, which could not be ignored.

The frenzy before and around Raphael was a hurricane of bodies, voices, and percussion instruments. Horses neighed and snorted, logs ground the earth flat with a steady *crunch*, and Kokhabel's damned retinue shrieked in ecstasy and fear.

"Kokhabel!" Raphael cried in the Still Small Voice.

The drums fell silent. Every head—serpentine, equine, or human—raised and cocked an ear. The crew dragging horses forward and hoisting at cables froze, except for a handful of men armed with goads struggling with an immense black horse in the very front of the bark's retinue. The animal bucked and snorted like it was stung, and its handlers, distracted by the Still Small Voice, tried hard to get the horse back under control without getting their skulls kicked open by its heavy hooves.

"Kokhabel!" Raphael cried again. The Still Small Voice sounded pathetically tiny in the sudden silence, but he knew it cut through everything, and every person in Washburn Fair Oaks Park heard it as clear as a ringing bell—a voice piercing to the center of each listener's private heart.

"Apep!" Kokhabel roared as he rose.

The bark lurched under the Fallen's feet like a loose, well-oiled skateboard, its deck tilting to one side and then the other as his immense feet thumped to the wood and then righting awkwardly as he stood. He turned and faced the Bearer of the Word, his former colleague, a heavy falchion in each hand.

Raphael tried not to give away his interest, but he notice the Marked Woman, bound and gagged, tumbling to the deck of the bark beside the fairy. Kokhabel's people hadn't even bothered to tie the fairy, who looked as broken and spineless as a rag doll and as white as bone. Eddie Marlowe stopped playing the tambourine and whirled, but a shaven-skulled man at each shoulder pressed a knife to his throat, and he grimaced in frustration.

Among the snake worshippers ran an orgy of the bloodletting damned. Raphael had a hard time telling the living from the dead in the jumble of carnage and carnality. Winged snakes hissed and darted forward, but they hung back in a collective curtain.

"Raphael," Kokhabel hissed with a low rasp in his throat. "You've come to join the party."

Raphael tried not to betray the unease he felt. The two sorcerers at Kokhabel's feet chanted and looked at him hungrily. One licked blood off his hooked knife.

"There is no place on earth for me," Raphael said, and as he said it, he realized the words were truer than he'd intended.

"Is there no place in Heaven?"

"Heaven is besieged," Raphael said. "It is no longer a place of rest, for those within or for those without."

Across the writhing multitude, he saw the blond hair of Enoch Emery. He almost missed the Son of Light because the man had thrown aside his parka and now calmly walked around the fringes of the crowd, naked among the naked. None of the snake cultists appeared to pay him any heed.

"Would Heaven even welcome you back?" Kokhabel's forked tongue flickered in and out of his mouth as he spoke, and he adjusted his grip in his swords' hilts.

"I haven't asked." That was more or less true. Heaven had approached him. "I need a body. This mortal earth crushes me."

"This is no place for a being of pure intelligence," the Fallen agreed. "The host of Heaven turns out to be a fragile and delicate thing."

Raphael pushed into the territory of brazen falsehood. "I want a body, Kokhabel," he said. "I beg you to take me in."

Enoch Emery shuffled closer to the roped horses. Winged snakes whipped around him in the chill air, but he drifted as calm and dazed-looking as any of Kokhabel's people. Casually, Raphael looked for Chuy and found him too. He had stripped down to jeans and stood panting at the edge of the crowd beside the church, the shotgun in his hands.

Kokhabel laughed. The noise sounded like the faint whisking burr of sandpaper over rough timber. "I once begged you to take me in," he reminded Raphael. "I even begged you to arrest me, to bring me to trial."

"And it's a good thing I didn't do it!" Raphael snapped. "If I had, you'd be in Heaven and under siege with the others!"

"It is a good thing," the Fallen agreed. "But you were wrong nonetheless."

Raphael hesitated, but he realized Kokhabel was right. He *had* been wrong. His own long exile on Earth, in Dudael and in the months since Jacob bar Azazel had harrowed and shattered Hell, weighed on him. Perhaps Kokhabel didn't feel the weight of the world in such a physical way, but exile must be painful for him anyway.

"You're right, Kokhabel."

"I'm right. But you must call me Apep."

Uh-oh. "That's the name under which these people serve you."

"It's also the name under which *you* will serve me."

Raphael nodded. What was taking Enoch Emery so long? The Son of Light was behind Kokhabel now—behind Apep—and out of Raphael's sight. The flying snakes hissed louder.

Kokhabel threw back his snakelike head and bellowed at the night sky. "My brother joins us!" he roared, and the crowd roared back at him. "Would you like a man's body?" he asked, gesturing with one sword at Eddie Marlowe, and then he gestured at the woman Qayna. "Or a woman's?"

Raphael heard confused grumbling behind the Fallen—not quite loud enough to be yelling. Enoch must be making his move.

He turned his attention to the two priests of Apep and Whispered. "Join me," he Whispered, and though the Whisper drained him of power, he still reveled in the warm, spiced smell of the winds of Eden—

Something slammed into him. Hard, cold, heavy, and reeking of death.

Raphael slipped. Dazed, he lost his grip on the air and fell.

Kokhabel laughed and leaped off the bark. Beneath him, copulating worshippers ceased their moaning and died, crushed and broken. The Fallen strode forward, slashing his weapons left and right through the air as if he was chopping a path through tall grass with machetes.

"Fool!" he snarled, and swung at Raphael.

Raphael recovered just in time to throw himself back and up. The tree trunk–sized blades snickered just short of him. Could they wound him? He would have thought not, but for the frozen blow he'd just taken from somewhere.

The cold buffeted him again even as he thought of it. He tumbled backwards, drifting.

Sorcery. Raphael was no expert in the subject—no Messenger could be, except at a theoretical level—but he didn't know what else could account for the pounding he was taking. He lurched spastically backward, trying not to be crushed under Apep's blows. But at least Enoch Emery was now mounted and charging his horse towards the bark.

The crowd reacted, but it was slow. Hands slapped at Enoch; he ignored them.

Raphael rose up and back, trying to get out of Apep's reach.

"Once, you could have joined us!" Apep shrieked as he charged. "That was a long, long time ago!"

His two nearest wizards chanted and raised their arms, staring at Raphael.

Enoch reached the bark and threw himself from the back of his horse, rolling onto the deck and crashing into the knees of one of Apep's wizards who held Eddie Marlowe prisoner. The bald man went down yelping, and suddenly the guitar player snapped around, a rigid hand chopping into the other wizard's Adam's apple.

Raphael tried to Whisper—

Carrion-reeking cold punched into him again.

He slammed into a tree his own size, and it rejected him soundly. The feel of the world's weight shifted for an instant from a general drag and crush on his whole being into a thundering hammer that pounded him to the earth.

Feet pounded on the grass of the park, and Raphael looked up.

Beyond Apap charging at him, two swords raised over his head, Raphael saw Eddie Marlowe. The black rock and roller and the fair Son of Light stood back-to-back on the deck of the bark. Eddie was whipsaw-thin, but he was fast, and he must punch hard, because at every blow he seemed to drop a cultist to the earth.

Raphael could flee, but it would do no good if Eddie Marlowe died on Apep's bark.

"Run!" he cried in the Still Small Voice.

In the momentary distraction while every head turned his way again, Eddie kicked a heavy man covered in snake tattoos right in the gut. The big man emitted a soft, surprised "Oomph" and disappeared over the edge of the boat.

Why were they not running?

Then Apep was upon him and Raphael rushed sideways, half flying and half rolling upon the cold, bruising earth.

Raphael threw himself between Apep's legs. To an outside observer it might have looked like a close fit and an outrageous risk, but Raphael was infinitely small—a mere point in the fabric of existence. He could have thrown himself between a terrier's legs just as easily, or a fly's.

Apep dropped to his knees, nearly pinning the Bearer of the Word as he crashed to the earth.

Raphael righted himself and danced out of reach of the scything falchions. He could move behind the Veil, but if he did, Apep would be free to focus on his escaping prisoner.

Hopefully Eddie was escaping.

Realizing that the bark's rolling logs were beneath him, Raphael flitted back and up. Snakes bit him, but their teeth were too small to hurt and too mortal to cut into him. Apep caught his sandaled foot on the foremost log and rattled out long curses in Infernal as he swayed on his feet and fell forward.

Raphael laughed—

And then shrieked as something stabbed him from behind.

He fell, rolling and tumbled away from the bark, the earth punching him heavily with every contact. At the rear of the bark he saw the two sorcerers of Apep who were still standing. One incanted, and the other raised his hooked knife.

Raphael ached, and he wondered what had stabbed him. The hooked knife was something unholy, something sorcerous. He tried to fly and couldn't. He felt … holed. Punctured. The infinite substance within him flowed out in a puddle of light.

Apep stood over Raphael and raised his swords.

"Aaagh!" The scream came from one of Apep's wizards, and the Fallen and the Bearer of the Word both turned to look.

Both shaved men staggered at the edge of Apep's bark and fell off, bouncing wetly among the rollers beneath it. Falling back into a ready stance from his roundhouse kick, Eddie Marlowe glared at Apep, then raised his arm and something brass-glittering and tinkling. The object sailed through the air, struck the Fallen in the chest, and then clattered to the ground.

It was a tambourine.

Enoch Emery, naked, bent over the Marked Woman, hacking at the ropes binding her hands and feet. She lay still, but Raphael recognized the look of cold fury in her eyes stabbing jets of hatred at the Fallen; he'd seen it before, and he knew she meant it.

Eddie turned and grabbed Twitch off the deck. The fairy yelped a soft, staccato whimper as he heaved her over his shoulder, and then Eddie sprinted away towards the prow of the ship. A naked man rushing him bare-handed from the side got Eddie's fingers jammed into his eyes for his trouble. A flying snake found itself yanked from the air and converted instantly into a bola, flung fangs-first into the crowd of worshippers.

Apep lunged after the guitarist. The Fallen nearly tripped on the rollers but then got his sandal soles onto the deck and caught his balance. He rushed forward with a roar—

Then staggered sideways.

Apep's bellow was so infuriated and so pained that for a moment, Raphael forgot that the snake-headed Fallen was a renegade, a rebel, a sorcerer, a willful apostate, a self-appointed deity, and apparently intent on murdering Heaven's first designated prophet in centuries. The wracked agony in the cry made Raphael remember Kokhabel, the wretch in a stolen body and beast's head fleeing from the men of Shet across his ruined adoptive city, broken Ainok.

Kokhabel, whose mistake was not much different from Raphael's. He had been unhappy with his lot, he had wanted something else, and he had rebelled against the will of Heaven to get it.

And now he fell, and Raphael saw that he fell because someone much smaller had thrown himself into his knee.

Thrown *her*self into his knee, Raphael corrected himself. It was the Marked Woman. Her black duster flapped behind her, and she flailed with one free arm, stabbing the hooked knife of one of Kokhabel's own priests again and again into the vulnerable flesh behind Kokhabel's knee.

He bellowed again and slapped at her with one hand. She held on, and together they lurched back and forth across the ship's deck.

Raphael rose slowly and in agony. Howls and murder erupted all across the writhing park. Eddie seemed to be on a horse and racing away, but in the wrong direction.

Boom! Boom!

Raphael turned to see Chuy. The man's task had been to give Eddie cover for getting away, but with Eddie racing in the wrong direction, Chuy charged around the periphery of the crowd. He had thrown aside the shotgun and now held a pistol in either hand. As Apep cultists and mutant semi-snake people recovered enough of their wits to charge him, he gunned them down.

Raphael couldn't be sure, but it looked like Eddie's horse was galloping towards the museum.

Maybe he knew the escape routes better than Raphael did. Maybe there was a car with a tank full of gas in the Institute, or a small-engine plane on its roof. At least Raphael could help.

"Kokhabel!" he yelled in the Still Small Voice. The effort nearly split him. He was afraid to look down at himself, afraid he would see dimmed glory, a weakening of the Heavenly matter that made him up.

Scaly faces hissed, and a wave of winged snakes turned and rushed in his direction.

Kokhabel snapped his shoulders around—

Lost his balance—

And fell.

SPULCH!

The Fallen impaled himself on the mast of his bark.

Blood spouted down in a red torrent, spattering on Enoch Emery, who rushed to the attack with a rough-ended spar in both his hands like a spear. He jammed the jagged, splintered butt of the wood into Kokhabel's hip and for his trouble got kicked to the ground.

Raphael dropped the Veil around himself—

Only it didn't come down.

He tugged at it again, and again felt a sudden, sharp stabbing. He looked down and saw two of Kokhabel's wizards. He had thought he was floating above ground, but he saw now that he was standing on the earth.

And one of the priests had his hooked knife inserted into Raphael's being.

Lines shimmered into view surrounding Raphael. They were lines of writing. He didn't know the characters, but the pattern was obvious enough. The lines made a ward of some kind, probably a ward of holding.

He tried to rise and couldn't. He tried to retreat and found himself stuck.

The second priest held his fists in the air and tugged. He looked like he was pantomiming pulling a net full of fish out of the sky, and the lines of visible writing jiggled and tightened with each yank.

"Oh, no," hissed the priest with the knife. Raphael saw that the man had no teeth and his tongue had been surgically—or sorcerously—forked. "You're not going anywhere."

CHAPTER NINE

Raphael managed not to scream. It didn't matter; Kokhabel screamed enough for both of them.

The iridescent net of words kept him from moving at all, except as the priest dragged him, and it kept him from slipping behind the Veil. It was heavy, too, and the weight of the world began to burn on the Bearer of the Word. Adding only insult, snakes nipped at him like gnats as he went.

The priests dragged him across the park. As he went, he saw Kokhabel rip himself free of the bark, yank the mast from his own chest and lay about himself like a dervish. He definitely hit the Marked Woman and he might have hit Enoch Emery too, and in his indiscriminate swoops and slashes, he flattened more than a few of his own followers. He didn't seem to notice their deaths. He boiled in a blood-stoked berserker rage, but Raphael felt only pity for the snake-headed abomination he could now only see as a kinsman.

Chuy Archuleta, with his brother Mike inside, raced for the Institute. He ran out of bullets before he made it, and then a gaggle of maenads with snakes for fingers and toes dragged him to the ground.

The world around Raphael pulsed, fading in and out. He cried out wordlessly in shock and surprise. He was perfectly used to sleep, inside the body of a vessel; he'd slept night after night for many years, sometimes for decades at a stretch in the empty wasteland of Dudael. But he'd never slept, never passed out, never lost consciousness, in his own native form.

Messengers of Heaven did not sleep.

Raphael didn't see what happened to Eddie. He focused on staying alert, fighting the feeling that he was a helium balloon with a slow leak and soon would be lying sad and limp on the ground.

The priests dragged him up the steps, past the ramp, tower, and altar. Something had happened to the tower, and it sagged heavily to one side. The altar had slid off the apex and lay upended on the marble steps. The naked prisoners stared at Raphael as he passed, expressions of dumb resignation cruelly metamorphosing into glimmers of hope and then shrapnel-blasted craters of black despair.

A corner of the wide front hall of the Institute had been welded over with a grill of thick iron bars, making it an ugly yet efficient cage. In the gloom, Raphael saw it only dimly, lit by firelight coming through the windows. Ahead of Raphael, burly men in filthy, torn pants dragged Eddie Marlowe. The guitar player still clutched Twitch the fairy, now in both arms, and continued to hold on to her as they threw him to the floor inside the cage. Chuy followed, screaming Spanish curses.

The men slammed the grill shut with a sound that echoed like thunder in the museum, pinning the door with three U-shaped bike locks. Raphael struggled to stay awake.

More men threw Enoch down. Not to the ground, but onto a waist-high slab of black stone with hieroglyphic writing on it. He punched and kicked, but there were too many of them.

Heavy footsteps. Raphael turned to look and saw Kokhabel lurching through the triple-tall front doors of the Institute. The Fallen held a hand to his side where the mast had impaled him, not entirely stanching a serious flow of blood that spilled over his fingers and dripped onto the floor.

Kokhabel jabbed a finger of his free hand at Raphael. "Bind them!" he hissed.

Even without his injury, Raphael might not have been able to resist the force of the net. He tried anyway, and the result was humiliating. With a simple twist of his wrist, the net priest tugged Raphael sideways and down, bringing him prone and on top of Enoch Emery.

Raphael hurt.

Kokhabel laughed, and Raphael had enough presence of mind to see that the Fallen was looking at Enoch Emery's wrist.

"A Son of Light! How *fitting* ..." He darted forward and stabbed down with one hand, slicing into Enoch's wrist.

Enoch bucked and screamed.

"This will not fade," Kokhabel hissed. It came out like a threat.

The Fallen held his own fist over Raphael and squeezed. Hot blood spattered on, around, and through Raphael, marking both him and the Son of Light who struggled for breath and freedom below him.

The knife priest set aside his weapon and came forward with a fragment of bone. Raphael tried to fight but couldn't, and then the needle stabbed him. He and Enoch screamed together.

"This stylus is the bone of Azazel," Kokhabel intoned.

His priests chanted, and Raphael couldn't understand their words. He felt shapes being drawn onto him and onto Enoch Emery's flesh at the same time.

"By the bone of Azazel, by his sin and by his will, I bind you."

Raphael jerked, grabbing for anything he could grab to pull himself free, and when he raised his arm the arm of Enoch Emery came with it. Someone wept, and he wasn't sure who. The ceiling of the Institute above him slowly rotated.

* * *

Someone sang.

> *If the price of compassion is my virtue,*
> *May all my sins lead to thee.*

And may thou in thy wisdom grant mercy
To a sinner who begs on his knees.
May thou who art the Lord of Lights
Light the path at my feet.
May thou whose hand guides the wanderer
Give direction to me.

Raphael opened his eyes in pain and in shadow. The singing stopped.

He was in a body, but it felt wrong.

He looked down at himself and saw Enoch's flesh. A jagged gash cut through the wrist where Enoch's tattoo had been, but there were new markings on the man's body. Red markings. Letters in Infernal that Raphael couldn't read, but they looked like curses. Kokhabel had tattooed Enoch with his own blood.

"He's waking up."

Eddie Marlowe shoved himself into Raphael's field of vision. He looked more haggard and food-deprived than ever, and even as their gazes met, Eddie's Infernal eye slid sideways, and he blinked hard.

"Tell me who you are," the guitar player said in a hard voice. Raphael saw that Eddie had a fist cocked back, ready to strike.

"Raphael," he said. "This body is borrowed. The man is Enoch Emery, and he is in the service of Heaven. And you're Eddie Marlowe. You and I met for the first time in Azazel's well of imprisonment, at the waters of Dudael."

"Dammit." Eddie sat back.

Raphael sat up. He was in Enoch Emery's body, all right, but it didn't respond right. The body had taken a beating, but that wasn't the problem. His connection with the body was wrong. It felt like having his left hand in a right-handed glove.

Chuy sat in the corner of the cage, and Twitch lay on the floor, a scrap of leather draped over her. Raphael pointed at it. "Is that it?"

"The Skin of Adam? The leather kilt God made for Adam when he threw him out of the Garden? Damned if I know. I thought it might be, but it isn't doing any good. Maybe none of us here have enough faith. The Marked Woman might be able to tell you, but she ain't here."

"I come Bearing the Word," Raphael said.

"What the hell are you talking about?"

"Heaven," Raphael said. "I come as a Messenger. I have a message for you, Eddie."

"If Heaven is using *you* as a Messenger," Eddie snorted, "shit must *really* have hit the fan."

"It must have," Raphael agreed, cracking an awkward smile, "or *you* wouldn't be getting a message."

Eddie laughed out loud at that. "Touché," he said. "When times are hard, you go with what you got."

"Truer words," Twitch whimpered from the floor, "et cetera."

Eddie stared at the fairy and furrowed his brow. "All right, then, let's hear it."

Raphael tried to release himself from Enoch's body and couldn't.

Eddie eyed him curiously. "There was a time I would have given any money for the baffled look on your face," he said. "But now I find it troubling."

"Not half as troubling as I do," Raphael said. He tried again.

Nothing. He remained in Enoch's body.

He tried a third time and fell back to the floor, gasping in pain, as something inside him tore.

"The tattoos," Eddie said. "You're stuck."

"That's not good news," Raphael groaned. "I'm Bearing the Word, and I can only Bear it to you in my Heavenly form."

"You can't just *say* it?" Eddie looked skeptical.

"The Word isn't just a message!" Raphael snapped. "It's an investiture. And the part of it that *is* words, I don't know. I didn't read the words; I ate them."

Eddie shook his head. "Why's it always gotta be a circus with you guys?"

"I don't make the rules," Raphael grumbled.

"You don't keep them, either," Eddie snorted.

"Look who's talking."

Eddie sighed and rubbed his eyes with the palms of his hand. "It probably doesn't matter. Whatever your message is, our history means I'd have to assume you're lying."

"It isn't just a message," Raphael repeated sourly. "It's an investiture."

"You said that already," Eddie agreed. "It didn't make sense the first time, either. You mean, like a robe? Like Elisha taking Elijah's cloak?"

Raphael nodded. "Like a robe," he agreed. "Like a mantle of authority."

That got the guitar player's attention. "Authority to do what?"

"I haven't heard the Word myself," Raphael reminded him. "It used to be that a prophet was called and sent forth when the king needed to be reminded of his indebtedness to and dependence on Heaven. And if you got the Word, you'd know I wasn't lying."

"A prophet?" Chuy laughed weakly.

"A king?" Eddie wasn't laughing. "Like our buddy Apep out there, king of Minneapolis?"

"Maybe."

"How can you not know?" Eddie squinted.

Raphael shrugged. "I Bear the Word. It doesn't come from me, it comes from the Chancellor. It's the same with Writs—I don't write them; I just execute them when tasked to do it."

"Why can't you guys ever make it easy?" Chuy asked.

"It isn't supposed to be easy," Raphael told him. "I think it's supposed to be a test. Not knowing everything in advance is part of the test."

"Hell of a test," Eddie said. "Everybody fails."

"There's repentance."

"Is there?" Eddie jumped to his feet, suddenly full of blazing energy. "I've seen Hell, Messenger. Maybe you forget— I see it all the time! It's *full!*"

"People can choose sin," Raphael said.

Doom, doom, da-doom, the drums outside started again.

"Are all those people in Hell murderers?" Eddie gestured towards the park and the flickering orange bonfire light creeping in through the Institute's high front windows. "Adulterers, idolaters, cannibals? Worshippers of Apep?"

Raphael said nothing.

"Don't get me wrong!" Eddie barked. "There's no bigger believer than me in the fundamental badness of human beings. Nor is there a bigger screw-up than me. I'm in a rock-and-roll band, remember? But we can't all be that bad! I've read the books—all of them. Hell, I can quote half of them from memory! It doesn't add up."

"The plan—" Raphael ventured.

"The plan is broken!" Eddie roared. "I don't know what happened, but the plan failed. We're at a dead end, a broken branch, a sterile stump, and a scorched earth, and the world ends in sharpened, bloody teeth."

"You're such a poet," Chuy said. Raphael couldn't tell whether he meant it as mockery.

"Yeah, well," Eddie muttered. "There's a reason I wrote all the songs."

"Not a poet," Raphael disagreed. "You sound like a prophet."

"You say potato," Twitch moaned. "You know."

"Stop it, Twitch," Eddie said. The words were brusque, but his tone was soft. "Adrian's gone."

Twitch shuddered. Close up, the fairy looked like her bones had been pulverized, rendering her a floppy sack of meat. "Do you think I don't know it? Only it turns out death's not quite the funny joke I used to think it was."

"No," said Raphael, realizing that the tearing sensation he felt inside was partly the same punctured, leaking feeling he'd felt before being forced into Enoch's body. "It isn't funny at all."

"What if I kill you?" Eddie asked.

Raphael scrambled back. "Is that a threat?"

Eddie squatted on his heels and held up his hands in a non-threatening gesture. "More like a hypothesis. You're stuck in a body. I hear you telling me you can't Bear the Word to me because of it. What if I freed you?"

"Do prophets kill people?" Chuy asked.

"Samuel hacked Agag to pieces at the altar because of Saul's disobedience," Eddie said, almost in a whisper. "Elijah killed four hundred priests for worshipping Baal. Maybe Eddie Marlowe can kill this guy to get the Word."

"I don't think that's a good idea," Raphael said slowly. He didn't like the idea of killing Enoch, who had risked so much and brought him so far. He was also acutely aware of the sensation that his light was dimming, slowly dissipating into the void, and he had a terrible nagging sensation that without Enoch's body, he might not survive.

He could barely even formulate the thought in his mind, and he certainly couldn't get his arms around his fears. Would he just *cease to exist?* "I think we should focus on getting out of here, and then figure out the … body problem."

Eddie spun suddenly and kicked the door of their cage with his combat boot. *Clang!* The grating jerked slightly, but only as far as its three U-shaped bicycle locks would permit, and then it fell back into its smug, indomitable place. Raphael looked around the shadowy hall and was relieved that there were no guards to hear the ruckus.

"Yeah?" Eddie pushed. "What did you have in mind? The bars are too close to worm through. Our sorceress is outside, captured, and probably being bled onto a pile of archaeological relics as we speak. Our fairy is broken. And the angel that was sent to us is stuck in a human body."

"Let me try," Raphael suggested.

Eddie nodded and shifted out of the way so Raphael could take his place by the door. Raphael scooted about to find his position of maximum leverage, with his legs wedged against the wall and his shoulder against the door. He kicked, kicked, and kicked again, but all he got for his trouble was more clanging noise and a bruise on his shoulder.

The iron was solid.

Eddie harrumphed.

"Could we tunnel with a spoon?" ventured Twitch.

"No damn spoon."

"How about teeth?" Chuy asked.

Eddie stared at him. "We can't tunnel with teeth, either, unless you've had a hell of a lot better dental work than I have."

Chuy shook his head. He was sweating despite the cold, and his face had a look of intense concentration. "No. I mean, someone could bite me."

"Oh, if only I were feeling just a tiny bit better." Twitch chuckled and shivered beneath the flap of leather.

"What the hell kind of home did you two grow up in?" Eddie harrumphed. "Mike asked the dumbest questions, but I'm starting to miss him anyway. He couldn't keep his mouth off the bottle, his fingers outta the cookie jar, or his eyes off the girls, but at least he never invited me to take a nibble!"

"I don't mean it like that." Chuy pushed himself to his feet, leaning against the stone wall in the corner of the room.

"Oh yeah? How did you mean it?"

"I meant … *really* bite me."

"Shame," Twitch groaned.

"Does this get us somewhere?" Eddie asked. "Or do you just like being punished for your sins so much you want another dose?"

Chuy looked at Raphael unsteadily. "You said the blood, right?" he asked. "The blood is like the name."

Raphael tried to think back to what he had said earlier that evening. "I believe I said that nobody understood these matters particularly well, myself included."

"Yeah." Chuy nodded. "But we gotta try, right? What we got to lose?"

"Okay," Eddie said, "I'll bite. What are you holy rollers talking about?"

Chuy ignored him and kept talking to Raphael. "You come in through the name, and that's like blood, and you come out through the name, and that's like blood. Right?"

"Yes," Raphael said, "as well as English can capture those ideas."

"Something wrong with English?" Eddie pushed.

Raphael shrugged. "It depends what you need a language for. English isn't Angelic. It isn't even Adamic."

"Your generosity is so disarming."

"Blood, though," Chuy insisted. "You come out of your body through the blood."

Raphael wondered what Chuy was getting at. "It isn't my body."

"Yeah, but the blood."

"The name. I come into and out of a human being through his name."

"Which is the same thing as the blood."

"In some sense. What are you thinking?"

Chuy jerked backward violently and leaning against the wall, juddering.

"Mike," Eddie whispered. "Keep it together, man."

Chuy threw himself to the ground and did push-ups.

"You're thinking you're going to leave Mike's body somehow," Raphael realized.

"Uh-huh," Chuy puffed, pushing up and down, up and down.

"And what? Escape?"

Chuy climbed to his knees, panting. "Screw that. I'm going to get us out of here."

"Those people out there are damned already," Eddie pointed out, his eye sliding sideways on the word *damned*. "You ain't gonna scare them into helping us."

"If I can get out through the blood, I can get in through it, too." Chuy's eyes glittered in the darkness. Outside, the drums and howling grew louder.

"I dunno." Eddie scratched his chin. "Mike could pick locks. That seemed a hell of a lot easier."

Chuy ignored him. "Just don't bandage my arm—*Mike's* arm—until I get back." He held his own forearm in his hand, sized it up, and then opened his mouth—

"Whoa!" Raphael called. It might be madness, but he didn't see a better option short of killing Enoch Emery, and that seemed like no option at all. "If you're going to do this, at least use my knife." He pulled the pocketknife from Enoch's jeans pocket.

"Oh, sure," Twitch laughed dryly. "*Now* you tell us you're armed."

Chuy didn't hesitate. He slashed his wrist, a long slice up one forearm that showed pink for a moment and then began to flow crimson.

It must have been a deeper cut than he'd intended, Raphael thought. Blood gushed out in a river.

"Dammit!" Eddie jumped forward and grabbed Chuy's forearm with both hands, covering the wound.

Chuy closed his eyes. "Don't ... bandage ... it ..." he murmured. Then he slouched forward into Eddie' arms.

"Chuy?" Eddie asked. "Chuy!"

Chuy collapsed, dragging the smaller Eddie with him to the floor. Blood spattered onto the stone, and Eddie patted around the cell. His hand landed on the leather flap covering Twitch. He snatched it up and pressed it to Chuy's wound. After a moment's consideration, he slid the leather back to avoid covering the entire injury, leaving just the end exposed to continue bleeding.

"Chuy?" he asked again.

The bigger man shook his head. "*Mierda*, I need a drink."

Chapter Ten

Eddie laughed. "Nothing to drink here." He jerked a thumb over his shoulder at the front door. "If you're lucky, you might get a whiff of what they're smoking just before they chop you to pieces on their altar. Numb the pain a little."

Raphael barely heard Eddie's words. He stared at the leather in Eddie's hands.

"Eddie," he said, and pointed.

Eddie looked. "Son of a bitch," he muttered. He climbed up into a squatting position.

"What is it?" Mike asked, and the bass player sat up.

Eddie pulled away the leather and showed him. There was no blood on it.

"Where's the blood?" Mike asked. Then he looked down at his own arm. "*Chingado.*" Most of the cut was closed and gone.

"It drank it up," Raphael said.

They all stared, including Twitch, who flopped slowly over onto her back to look up at the folds of leather.

"Maybe it *is* the Skin of Adam," Eddie muttered.

The leather trembled.

"Put it on," Raphael suggested.

Mike shuffled away in a crouch. "Don't heal the cut all the way, Chuy said."

"You're liking your brother that much, huh?" Eddie asked.

"It isn't about *liking* him."

"I didn't mean on you," Raphael said. He pointed at Twitch.

Twitch shrank back as far as she could, which, since she was lying on the floor, wasn't much. "I'm feeling a little less sure about this now," she said.

"We walked all the way from Illinois," Eddie growled. "Now that we know we got the right old relic and that the damn thing works, you're gonna back out on me? I don't think so, fairy." But he didn't force the skin on Twitch. He just held it up between them.

Where it quivered.

Doom, doom, da-doom.

Twitch looked into Eddie's eyes and finally nodded. "I'll need help," she said.

Raphael and Mike moved in, and all three of them helped the fairy. She winced at the softest touch, so Raphael was as gentle as he could be, peeling off the spiked black leathers and setting them aside. Twitch looked like a young woman who had been run over by a truck—she was bruised and battered, and where ribs and kneecaps should have given her body points of crisp definition, instead it sagged and collapsed. She yelped once as Mike accidentally pinched her tail.

When they had undressed her, Eddie pulled the Skin of Adam down over her head. It fit loosely, though to Raphael's eye it seemed to tighten slightly once it was on. Then Eddie shooed the others away, cradling Twitch against his chest as if to protect her modesty.

A deep, rough laugh pulled Raphael's gaze away.

Four men, or creatures that had once been men, crossed the shadowed vault of the Institute's front hall. In the lead came a figure that might have been a miniature version of Apep, with the same snake's head on a man's body, white kilt, and sandals. A favored priest, maybe? He even wore two long hunting knives in his belt, which made him look like a weak imitation of his Fallen god.

Behind the priest came two naked men. As they got closer, even in the dim light Raphael could see that they had the smooth, scaled skin of reptiles, and one of them had a long tail swishing back and forth behind him on the floor. They were both armed, one with a sawed-off shotgun and the other with a two-by-four with long nails poking through. At the rear of the small procession came a thin man with a jagged face. Snakes sprouted from his shoulders like a living collar or a writhing, scaly scarf of flesh, and he limped slightly on one bloody leg.

"Your sorceress has a lot of blood in her," Snake Head chortled. "Well, *had*. Your turn now."

Eddie laid Twitch on the floor and stood. Shotgun pointed his weapon at the guitar player, and Nail Club raised his like a baseball bat, ready to whack anyone who came through the door without authorization. Snake Collar moved in close behind them, grinning like a ghoul with a secret.

Raphael tensed the borrowed muscles of Enoch Emery's body, preparing to join in the charge he knew Eddie Marlowe would have to make.

Snake Head opened all three bike locks with three keys and stepped aside. Eddie barged into the door, curling the fingers of his hands into a half-fist—

At the same instant, Shotgun and Nail Club both screamed. Every snake on Snake Collar's shoulders snapped at once, biting the two men in front of him in multiple spots on their heads, necks, and upper arms.

Eddie snatched away Shotgun's weapon and swung it like a club, smashing a deep dent into Snake Head's snout with a single blow of the gun's butt. The bitten men sank to the floor without further cry, spastically jerking for a few seconds before holding still. Before he had hit the ground, Snake Head took two more jabs from Eddie's shotgun, both in the throat. He landed with a pinched screech and moved no more.

Raphael pushed through and grabbed the fallen two-by-four.

Snake Collar stepped back and raised his hands. "It's me, Chuy." He had a long, bloody gash in one side.

"How festive those snakes make you look," Eddie chuckled. "Not to mention the fact that Mike doesn't have a poisonous bite attack. You traded up."

"I ain't staying like this, *hijo de puta*." It was a stranger's voice and a mutant's body, but the man still sounded all Chuy. He jabbed a finger at Mike, who raised his hands defensively. "You keep that wound open. I'm coming back as soon as we're out of this."

"This just gets weirder and weirder," Eddie grumped.

"Does that make you uncomfortable, Eddie?" Chuy the snake man asked. "I suppose you'd better not look behind you."

Raphael turned. Twitch stood, dressed again in her black leathers. She held out a handful of long silver fibers to Eddie.

Eddie cocked his head to one side and frowned. "Your tail?"

"I'll need a patch when we have the time," she said. "A girl doesn't like to feel that much breeze on her nethers."

"You're done," Raphael realized. "We can find the back way and get out of here. We'll ... figure out how to get me free of this body, and I can Bear you the Word."

"Not without Jane." Eddie snapped open the shotgun and checked the shells in both barrels. "When are you going to learn this, angel? We don't leave people behind."

"You left Jacob behind."

Eddie snapped the gun shut. "No, we didn't," he said. "Jim quit." He turned and walked towards the door of the Institute.

"She can't die," Raphael reminded the guitar player, following behind the others. He had a flash of memory as he said it, recalling the ink pot and the tattooing of the Marked Woman millennia earlier. "Remember? She'll get out sooner or later. You're talking about the woman who lived through the Flood by just drowning for forty days."

"She can't die," Eddie agreed, "but they can torture her. Have you considered the possibility that I might find that unacceptable?"

Raphael sighed, then opened his mouth—

Eddie pivoted and pointed the shotgun at his head. "Don't even try it, Bearer, or we'll be testing out the kill-the-messenger theory after all. Twitch?" he called over his shoulder. "How about a little avian reconnaissance?"

There was a moment of silence. "I can't," the fairy told him.

Eddie looked at his boots and shook his head. "Sorry, Twitch."

"Ah, well," the child of Mab sighed. "Life's hard. And then you live forever."

"I can tell you what's out there," Chuy offered. "They got Jane tied down on the snake altar on top of the wooden tower. They keep cutting her, and her blood runs down on all that pile of stuff under the altar."

"The mutants?" Eddie asked. "The snake worshippers?"

"Crowded all around. Close."

"Her gun?"

Chuy nodded, the snakes around his head bobbing disconcertingly up and down. "I looked for that, man. Didn't see it."

Eddie crept to the edge of the door and peered outside.

Doom, doom, da-doom.

"This might be suicide," Eddie observed, "but I have an idea."

"Suicide is not a problem," Chuy said. "I've snuffed it before, and the asshole whose body I'm in pretty much deserves it."

"It's like this." Eddie pointed, and Chuy slipped around Eddie's shoulder to get a good look. "You walk up there and untie her. Then you run away."

"And lead them right to us?" Mike asked.

"Don't worry, chickenshit," Chuy snapped back. "I'll lead 'em in the other direction."

Raphael edged around the others to get a look, Twitch at his side. The bonfires still blazed, but most of the park was now empty, the crowds squeezing against the Institute's steps on the near side of the open space. The Twin Cities lay around the Institute in a dark, sprawling ruin. The drums beat faster than ever, *doom, doom, da-doom,* and Kokhabel stood over the altar tower, leaning on the broken mast of his bark like a crutch. Below him, two of his kilt-clad priests stood over the altar, stabbing down with knives.

The unresisting body on the altar top, Raphael realized, belonged to Qayna.

"What if you get caught?" Mike asked.

"This is rock and roll," Eddie said. "You lose your place, you improvise—the louder, the better." He grabbed Chuy by the shoulder and shoved him forward.

Raphael tried again to emerge from Enoch Emery's body and failed. Biting back curses, he followed after Chuy.

Eddie stopped him with a raised hand. "I thought you wanted to Bear the Word to me."

"Yes," Raphael agreed. "And I thought you said the Marked Woman was more important." He pushed past Eddie and kept walking. Hopefully no one would notice the big, red tattoos on Enoch's chest—or at least would think nothing of them.

The crowd pulsated and roared around the base of the scaffold. Raphael walked forward with head high like he belonged. In their ecstatic madness, the worshippers of Kokhabel tore at each other, bit each other, and sometimes ripped each other limb from limb. If there was a difference between them and the damned, Raphael couldn't see it.

Chuy walked out onto the scaffold. Raphael followed him. As they drew closer to the altar, he saw the Marked Woman's blood. It wasn't the amount that was so unusual, he realized; what was unusual was that a person could lose that much blood and still be alive.

Not unusual—unique.

And though he had only executed the Writ given to him, Raphael still burned with shame at his involvement in her curse. He was responsible. How could he tell himself otherwise?

Chuy stopped walking halfway along the scaffold. Raphael almost bumped into him, and swayed back as the collar of snakes hissed and snapped.

"What is it?" he whispered.

"Eleven o'clock, low."

Chuy resumed walking forward, and Raphael looked down.

Beneath the scaffold was a pile of stuff, all of it antique and much of it probably just garbage. But among the suits of armor, swords, cups, tapestries, sandals, clay tablets, coins, and books, he saw what Chuy had seen—the Calamity Horn. The puny, doom-laden pistol of Gavrilo Princip, an FN Model 1910. A nothing of a gun by modern standards, but in the Marked Woman's hands, Raphael had seen it dish out mayhem to a squadron of Bearers of the Sword. The Calamity Horn was cursed. One aspect of its curse was that only its maker, the Marked Woman, could fire it. Another was that its report caused madness. A third was that it had the power—Raphael had once thought it the unique power, though now he wasn't so sure—to destroy immortal beings.

It lay inside a conquistador's helmet, spattered with Qayna's own blood dripping onto it from above. Around it, Kokhabel's worshippers rutted like battling mountain goats, hurling each other against the ground and against the rough wooden beams jammed under the scaffolding.

Raphael turned from following Chuy and jogged down the stairs. He kicked aside a dazed man who clutched and groped at his leg, aware that Chuy, above him, was halfway along the ramp. He pushed between two clinging women as Chuy approached the altar. He dragged a wild-eyed cannibal away from feasting on the intestines of a screaming man and gave the cannibal an uppercut to the jaw with so much force he heard the man's teeth shatter.

Sometimes, being a Bearer of the Word inside a vessel was very satisfying.

The cultists paid him no mind; he wasn't doing anything to them that they weren't doing to each other.

"Aaaaaaagh!" The scream came from above him, and Raphael knew that Chuy had arrived. A snake-headed, kilt-clad priest slammed to the ground immediately in front of him, crushing two naked worshippers into an indistinguishable knot of elbows and sweat.

Surrounded by the bloodthirsty, the lustful, and the mad, Raphael stooped and picked up the Calamity Horn. He looked up and saw the Marked Woman, wobbling to her feet next to Snake Collar Chuy.

Kokhabel bellowed, rising from his crutch in sudden realization of what was happening. He lurched forward—

"Qayna!" Raphael called in the Still Small Voice, and he threw the Horn straight up—

The drums fell silent—

Kokhabel slammed into the edge of the tower, sending shattered timbers flying in all directions. Chuy's borrowed body disappeared in the destruction. Qayna turned and leaped at the last possible instant. Her duster flared out around her like wings, snapping in the cold night air as she reached out and snatched the pistol in midair.

Raphael couldn't take his eyes off her. She sailed gracefully, turning as she flew and pointing her gun backward behind her.

Kokhabel's altar collapsed as he waded through the scaffold. Relics, garbage, and naked human bodies flew in all directions, propelled by his massive feet.

Bang! Bang! Bang!

Qayna fired.

The orgy of blood around Raphael exploded.

"Stop!" he Whispered, but the warm winds of Eden were snuffed out by the frozen hurricane of murderlust. Hands and teeth bore down on Raphael, seizing him, tearing him.

Enoch Emery died almost instantly, and suddenly Raphael was rising out of the dead man's name and into the air.

He saw Eddie Marlowe rushing out the front door of the Institute. Mike—or was it Chuy again?—came on his heels with the two-by-four in his hands, and Twitch followed them, holding two long knives. She looked wrong, he thought, without her tail. He wondered what had happened to her. What had the Skin of Adam done?

He didn't know what it had done to Adam. He'd met Adam and his family only after Azazel's rebellion. Someone knew, and a small part of the being that was Raphael resolved to find out.

But he could again feel the puncture and the leak. It was a torrent of light now, and it burned.

Qayna crashed to the ground in the frenzied crowd, kicking and cursing.

Kokhabel charged forward, swinging the ship's mast down over his head like a sledgehammer.

Raphael turned in midair to face Eddie Marlowe. Feeling himself dissipating into the world's void and hearing the worshippers of Kokhabel dissolve into animal rage beneath him, Raphael Bore the Word.

EDDIE MARLOWE!

Eddie fell to the ground in astonishment. His shotgun blast went wide and unheard in the sudden roaring river-rush, the thundering cacophony of time-splitting sound and glory that was the Bearing of the Word. Mad revelers beneath Raphael screamed in pain and terror as his light and glory became a burning fire, rebounding off the stone walls of the Institute. Snakes burnt to ash as the flames touched them.

FEAR NOT.

"Holy shit!" Eddie yelled.

Mike staggered back into the Institute's door, sweeping Twitch along with him.

THIS IS THE WORD OF THE LORD UNTO YOU, EDDIE MARLOWE. REPENT AND SERVE THE LORD YOUR GOD.

Eddie dropped his gun. He knelt on the steps of the Institute, beneath massive stone columns, and tears streamed down his face. The roaring of the Word drowned out the world and the crowd and Kokhabel's bellowing, leaving a stillness at the center of which Raphael heard the soft, wet *plop* of Eddie's first tear hitting the stone.

"I am a man of unclean lips," he murmured.

Then the fire of the Word swallowed Eddie too. The thick smell of incense, anointing myrrh, and light engulfed them as if they were on the Stairway and not merely in front of the Minneapolis Institute of Arts. Eddie glowed and trembled, but his flesh didn't burn.

IT IS A GENERATION OF UNCLEAN LIPS, EDDIE MARLOWE. WHOM SHALL I SEND?

Raphael chose none of these words. They poured out of him unbidden. He hung suspended, trembling as much as Eddie did, and the Word burned through him.

Eddie bowed his head. "Send me."

Unseen trumpets sounded an inescapable *ALLELUIA.*

THE KINGDOM OF HEAVEN SUFFERS VIOLENCE, EDDIE MARLOWE. SEEK THE ARM OF THE LORD AND THE ENSIGN TO THE NATIONS. TAKE WITH YOU THE MARKED WOMAN, THE SONS OF THUNDER, AND THE CHILD OF ADAM.

Eddie looked up, yellow light blazing from his face even as it blazed upon him. "Where?" he asked. "What's the Arm of the Lord? The Ensign to the Nations? I don't understand. Send me, but I don't know where to go."

THE TWELVE GATES ARE BESIEGED, EDDIE MARLOWE. YOU MUST FREE THEM. THERE MUST BE A GREAT AND LAST SACRIFICE, THAT THE WORLD MAY BEAR THE NAME AND BE HEALED.

"What name?" Eddie asked. "Help me!"

FEAR NOT, the Word thundered through Raphael. *LO, I AM WITH YOU ALWAYS, EVEN UNTIL THE END OF THE WORLD.*

And then the Word was gone.

Raphael heard shrieking again. It came to him slowly at first, a sound that was far away. The incense hadn't dissipated, he realized, and light still seemed to bathe him.

He felt weak. Empty.

He heard the deep neighing of an angry horse, and then the Marked Woman's big black animal clattered up the steps past him. Qayna rode the beast, and the worshippers of Kokhabel scattered before her.

Raphael didn't see the Fallen.

The Stairway. He was still on the Stairway.

Eddie looked at him, and Raphael couldn't read the man's expression.

"Are you leaving?" Eddie asked him.

"I don't know," Raphael murmured. He tried to rise from the earth but couldn't. The Stairway at least drove back the damned, leaving a circle of light and sweet-smelling smoke around him and the new Prophet of the Lord. "Maybe. Are you?"

Eddie nodded. "I guess I have a job to do."

Raphael gasped. The world beyond the Stairway didn't disappear, but it seemed impossibly remote. Mike (and Chuy?) and Twitch stood and watched in apparent awe, but an indifferent and pragmatic Qayna gathered horses. "Do it well, Eddie," he said. "The service of Heaven is hard but sweet."

Eddie laughed grimly. "And the alternative is Hell. Are you ... dying?"

"I don't know." Raphael heard the *ALLELUIA* of the trumpets again. "Perhaps I am being summoned back." He could feel himself almost gone, but this time, he went without fear. If he ceased to exist, at least the weight of the world would no longer crush him. Kokhabel had been broken by the weight of the world, Raphael now saw, though in a different way than Raphael. And Azazel, too. "If I am to return to Heaven, I will speak for them," he said.

Eddie frowned. "The snake worshippers?"

"Them too. Sinners. The Fallen. All of them. They deserve an advocate."

"You got your work cut out for you, then. There's a lot of sinners."

"We're all sinners."

Eddie nodded. "I'd help you, but it sounds like I got my own job to do."

And then Eddie Marlowe was gone, and the world with him.

About the Author

D.J. (Dave) Butler is a novelist living in the Rocky Mountain northwest. His training is in law, and he worked as a securities lawyer at a major international firm and in house at two multinational semiconductor manufacturers before taking up fiction writing.

Dave writes speculative fiction for all audiences. In addition to his steampunk, urban fantasy, and science fiction novels published with WordFire Press, he has a steampunk fantasy series published by Knopf; start following The Extraordinary Journeys of Clockwork Charlie with *The Kidnap Plot*. He is also the author of the epic fantasy *Witchy Eye* (Baen, forthcoming).

Dave is a lover of language and languages, a guitarist and self-recorder, and a serious reader. He is married to a powerful and clever woman, and together they have three devious children.

Read about Dave's writing projects at:
http://davidjohnbutler.com.

If You Liked ...

If you liked *Earth Angel,* you might also enjoy:

Quincy J. Allen

Chemical Burn
Blood Ties

Josh Vogt

Enter the Janitor
Maids of Wrath

Other WordFire Press Titles by D.J. Butler

City of the Saints
Crecheling

Rock Band Fights Evil
Hellhound on My Trail
Snake Handlin' Man
Crow Jane
Devil Sent the Rain
This World Is Not My Home
The Good Son

Our list of other WordFire Press authors and titles is always growing.
To find out more and to see our selection of titles, visit us at:

wordfirepress.com

www.ingramcontent.com/pod-product-compliance
Lightning Source LLC
Chambersburg PA
CBHW030414120726
47904CB00007B/2278